'Grow up, Abby,' Max muttered.

'You seem to have got it into your head that I'm some sort of rapacious animal on the prowl, whereas all I'm do
that it's the male'
female. Corny as
have too much
conning them into
not.'

Dear Reader

This month, I would like to ask you to think about the kind of heroine you would like to find in our stories. Do you think she should be sweet and gentle, on the look-out for a man who will be able to care for and nurture her, or should the heroine be able to give as good as she gets, throwing punch for punch, and quite capable of standing up for herself? If you have any opinions on this matter please let us know, so that we can continue to give you the books you want to read!

The Editor

Kate Proctor is part Irish and part Welsh, though she spent most of her childhood in England and several years of her adult life in Central Africa. Now divorced, she lives just outside London with her two cats, Florence and Minnie (presented to her by her two daughters who live fairly close by).

Having given up her career as a teacher on her return to England, Kate now devotes most of her time to writing. Her hobbies include crossword puzzles, bridge and, at the moment, learning Spanish.

Recent titles by the same author:

BITTERSWEET YESTERDAYS

A TEMPORARY AFFAIR

BY

KATE PROCTOR

MILLS & BOON LIMITED
ETON HOUSE, 18-24 PARADISE ROAD
RICHMOND, SURREY TW9 1SR

First published in Great Britain 1993
by Mills & Boon Limited

This edition 1993

ISBN 0 263 78175 5

Set in Times Roman 10 on 12 pt.
01-9308-53326 C

Made and printed in Great Britain

CHAPTER ONE

ABBY GRANTHAM glanced at her watch after replacing the telephone receiver on the desk before her. She had been on the telephone for the best part of an hour in her attempts to reason with Lady Morrison, she noted irritably.

Her growing frustration spilling over into a groan of exasperation, Abby leapt to her feet, her wide-spaced green eyes flashing ominously as she strode from her office, through the empty reception area and towards the double doors leading to her employer's office.

It was as she reached out both hands towards the heavy brass knobs, with the intention of flinging open the doors and marching in, that Abby found herself freezing to stillness.

'No!' she groaned aloud. This time she wasn't going to chicken out, she told herself angrily. This time, no matter which of his unpredictable moods Max Bradley happened to be in, she was going to have it out with him.

She took a deep breath, then flung open both doors, her eyes widening in shocked disbelief as they met the shambles to which the celebrated cartoonist had reduced his sister Jennifer's once ordered office.

'My God, what have you done to the place?' gasped Abby, her eyes flickering in horror over the wads of discarded drawing paper littering the pale green of the thick-pile carpet before coming to rest in puzzlement on the easel standing to the left of Jennifer Bradley's huge desk.

'Damn—he's not even here!' she groaned to herself, turning frustratedly on her heel.

'He is, but he's busy,' contradicted a drawling, disembodied voice, making her jump with fright.

Abby spun round and took tentative steps further into the room.

'Where are you?'

Max Bradley's dark, somewhat tousled head rose to view from behind his sister's desktop, the unwelcoming scowl adorning his features doing little to mar their startlingly good looks.

This time there was hostile impatience in the luminous blue of the luxuriantly lashed eyes peering over the desktop at her, Abby noted, and was reminded of the infinite variety of expressions of which those eyes were capable—and to what disconcerting effect.

'Well—what do you want?' he asked, rising to his full height from behind the desk.

Max Bradley was a tall, beautifully built man, his broad-shouldered, lean-hipped body more in keeping with that of a professional athlete than that of a highly successful cartoonist.

'I want to know what's going on in this place,' replied Abby exasperatedly.

'I'm hardly the person to ask,' drawled Max unconcernedly and promptly disappeared from sight once more. 'Try asking Julie what's her name, the one who manages the office.'

'Julie Moore's got her hands full just trying to keep things ticking over,' exclaimed Abby, marching round the desk to where she found him on all fours and deep in concentration over a series of sketches arranged on the floor beside him. 'And I honestly doubt if she has any more idea than anyone else as to what's going on,' she added, striving desperately not to let her words deteriorate into a shriek of exasperation as she was forced to address the silk-shirted breadth of his back. Accepting she was getting nowhere, she tried another tack. 'Your sister has a reputation second to few in the field of interior design.' Which was why she, as a newly qualified design student, had felt she was on cloud nine on getting a job with her, Abby reminded herself and immediately found herself fighting her inevitable feelings of guilt as she remembered how short-lived that euphoria had been. 'Don't you care that her reputation could be in jeopardy? And don't try telling me it's nothing to do with you,' she continued doggedly, determined to have her say. 'You can't honestly expect anyone to believe that it was simply coincidence that you turned up here just as Jennifer took sudden leave!'

He sat back on his heels, swivelling his body round to gaze up at her from eyes that were now disconcertingly inscrutable.

'So—what's your problem, green-eyes?'

'My name happens to be Abby,' she informed him from between clenched teeth.

'But that doesn't alter the fact that your eyes are a bewitching green,' he murmured mockingly, 'nor, for that matter, that you've hair like the leaves of autumn—copper and gold and——'

'For heaven's sake, this is ridiculous!' exploded Abby, turning angrily on her heel, then letting out a shriek of indignation as her ankle was encircled by lean brown fingers that instantly halted her flight.

'You find it ridiculous that I should compare your hair to the wonder of autumn leaves?' he enquired, his words soft with false innocence. 'I'm a man with a streak of romanticism in me a mile wide—or hadn't you realised that?' he added, his eyes now gazing up at her with a look she had quickly learned he could adopt at will and one she considered suitable only for a bedroom, while his hand began sliding purposefully up her leg.

Momentarily stunned to inaction by sheer disbelief, Abby, as though mesmerised, watched that lean, tanned hand disappear beneath the material of her skirt.

'Just what the hell do you think you're doing?' she shrieked, galvanised into reaction by her body's disconcertingly pleasurable response to the tingling warmth now at her knee.

The lascivious look in his eyes was replaced by one of deceptively boyish teasing as he removed his hand and grinned up at her.

'Sorry, my curiosity seems to have got the better of me,' he chuckled, his tone completely devoid of any repentance.

'Your curiosity?' queried Abby scathingly, and immediately took several reflex steps back as he rose agilely to his feet.

'Yes, curiosity,' he murmured, batting his eyes at her in a parody of innocence as he stepped towards her and gazed down at her. 'Stockings or tights—which is it?'

'I beg your pardon?' croaked Abby, convinced she had misheard.

'Which do you wear?' he expanded obligingly. 'Stockings or tights?'

'It's none of your damned business!' squeaked Abby in outrage.

'No more, I suppose than the running of my sister's business,' he murmured, casually reaching out and running his fingers through the thick, shoulder-length hair, the colour of which he had so accurately described only moments before.

Furious with herself for the inescapable *frisson* of excitement his touch had aroused in her, Abby angrily slapped aside his hand.

'It's clear I'm wasting my breath in attempting to appeal to your better nature—you obviously don't possess one!'

The instant she tried to move away, his hands descended on her shoulders.

'But *you* do—is that what you're saying?' he asked with silky softness. 'It's your better nature, is it, that accounts for this dedicated concern of yours for my sister and her business?'

Abby was disconcerted to feel hot colour rise in her cheeks.

'Why can't you simply listen to what I have to say,' she asked, and was immediately unsettled by the decidedly defensive tone in her words, 'instead of continually resorting to sarcastic flippancy whenever I try speaking to you?'

'Perhaps you're simply not trying to say the right things to me,' he murmured, that sultry bedroom look once again smouldering in his eyes as his hands began sliding in slow seduction from her shoulders to her upper arms.

'Oh, yes?' enquired Abby scathingly, appalled by the melting warmth suddenly pulsating lazily through her. 'Such as confirming your opinion that you're God's gift to women—is that the sort of thing you had in mind?'

'Perhaps,' he conceded, a half-smile curving his lips. 'But you'd have to put it a trifle more subtly than that—otherwise I might start having doubts as to your sincerity.'

'Needless to say, those women around here, with whom you flirt with such dedicated ease, wouldn't be entitled to any doubts as to your sincerity!'

'Certainly not—they're fully aware that there's flirting and flirting,' he replied in tones of mild rebuke, while his eyes enveloped hers in the smoky blue of their mesmerising gaze, 'and that most of the time it's no more than a light-hearted, two-way exchange between the sexes with nothing offered or demanded by either party.'

'Well, that's certainly not the way I'd describe the way you flirt,' exclaimed Abby indignantly, sensing instantly that she would have been wiser to remain silent, then knowing so with total conviction when his laughter began dancing softly around her, tingling against her skin like a physical caress.

'I'm glad you noticed,' he chuckled, his movements so lazily confident as he began drawing her into his arms that she was barely aware of his intention, 'because with you I shall be most demanding,' he added huskily, a sultry darkness glittering hypnotically in those heavy-lidded eyes as he drew her fully against him and began lowering his head to hers.

She felt the breath catch sharply in the back of her throat as her mind seemed to disintegrate into a chaos of confusion in the midst of which remained only one minute area of stark clarity. It was that core of sanity still remaining intact within her that turned her head in avoidance of that firm, full-lipped mouth so confidently seeking hers. It began fading with the breath of his laughter on her cheek and the touch of his hand against the nape of her neck and faded further as his fingers sank into the silken softness of her hair, coaxing her head round towards those waiting, laughing lips.

At seventeen she had almost managed to convince herself she was in love for the first time. Any enjoyment she had experienced when they had shared their first kiss had been swiftly marred by the sudden and inexplicable—and in no way welcomed—conviction assailing her that, much as she was attracted by him, this was not a man she had lost or ever would lose her heart to. And so it had always been, though often several kisses later than the first; that intuitive certainty would sooner or later rear up unbidden from within her and inevitably the relationship would end.

That one small area of clarity in the confusion of her mind, as Max Bradley's mouth had sought hers, had, most inexplicably, centred on a belated acknowledgement that, all in all, that much resented intuition might well have been a blessing in disguise.

It was Max's kiss, its initial teasing lightness flaring swiftly to hot, uncompromising demand, that drove any last fleeting thought from her mind, affecting her as no other kiss ever had with the contagious recklessness of its ardour.

She had no idea whether it was his arms tightening so fiercely around her, or hers around him, that brought their bodies so close that they were melting almost as one in the openness of a flagrant hunger—and nor did she care. Her entire being was lost in the magnitude of the delicious new sensations being unleashed with such explosive potential from a secret source somewhere deep within her, while her mouth, which only moments before had sought escape, parted in ecstatic welcome to the lips now plundering and exploring it with such aggressive passion.

Their bodies moving in fevered unison, he tilted her back against the desk, the lean, hard contours of his body against hers blatantly reiterating the impatient demands of the mouth exploring hers in an impetuous, bruising hunger that was awakening in her a need that seemed to sear through her veins like drug-laden, liquid fire.

'Abby!' he groaned in a hoarse, oddly pleading protest that reached her ears almost in the same instant that sanity had begun struggling to assert itself over the drunken madness possessing her.

'I...we'd better try unravelling ourselves,' she croaked in a breathless, distorted voice she barely recognised as her own, convinced she was asking the impossible of two bodies fused as though into one by the passion still raging through them.

'"Try" being the operative word,' he managed in a voice every bit as unrecognisable as hers.

Abby held the breath in her already over-taxed lungs as she sensed the battle momentarily storming within him, still impossibly holding it as a steely tension seemed to enter him, signalling that reason had finally won.

As he released her, drawing swiftly away from her, Abby found herself having to close her mind to any thought of what might have been had reason not prevailed, a shiver almost of fear rippling through her in that moment before her mind responded fully.

'It's safe to open your eyes now.'

At the sound of those drawling words Abby's eyes flew open—not that she had been in the least aware they were closed. Max was now seated on his sister's black leather executive chair, his expensively shod feet hooked nonchalantly around the base of the chair, one of the rollers of which, she noticed, had caught up and crumpled a couple of the sketches laid out on the floor.

Though her mind and body were reeling as though both had just been involved in an unimaginable disaster, it was on that crumpled paper that Abby's mind now fixated itself, eagerly embracing the distraction it afforded.

Her eyes flew to his, her only thought to warn him of the damage being done to his work; then everything in her froze. She instinctively knew she had caught him completely unawares in that instant in which their eyes met. Before, when she had witnessed desire in men's eyes, it had been a hunger diluted by a rueful acceptance of being doomed never to be assuaged. There was no such dilution to be found in the granite glitter of the desire fast fading in Max's eyes and her every instinct warned her that the rueful softness of accepted defeat was something she would never encounter in the steely blue of those heavy-lidded eyes which, even as she watched, had changed to a smouldering impatience.

She had realised from the start that his occasional bouts of jokey flirtation with all and sundry were no more than a minute facet of a more complex than most personality. As would most women finding themselves strongly attracted to a new acquaintance, she had looked for clues to what lay beneath the surface of that to which she was so drawn. With Max Bradley, she had quickly found, she hadn't far to look; he was easygoing and friendly only to a point and those who made the mistake of stepping beyond that point quickly found themselves encountering a chillingly remote, disturbingly dark side of him. Only now was she prepared to admit that she had sensed the powerful sensuality that was part of that darker side of him, and that, far from lessening the initial attraction she had felt towards him, it had strengthened it.

Oblivious of what she was doing, she shook her head, unable to accept what she was admitting to herself.

'It's pointless shaking your head,' he growled, scowling hostilely across at her. 'It didn't get nearly as out of hand as it could have.'

Abby was startled and more than a little disturbed by how much comfort she was deriving from how rattled he seemed by the extent to which things had got out of hand anyway. It was almost as though he was admitting that he hadn't been entirely in control—something to which he was plainly unused. She was racking her brains for something light-hearted and dismissive to say when he suddenly leapt to his feet with a muttered oath, lifted the chair from his work and crouched down to examine it minutely.

'Will it be all right?' Abby heard herself ask, her voice still not wholly recognisable.

His grunted reply left her none the wiser.

Stifling an exclamation of impatience, she glanced down at the glossy dark head perusing the drawings and instantly found her senses bombarded by the memory of those brief, erotically charged moments in his arms.

'All I wanted was for you to listen to what I had to say!' she exploded, appalled by the chaos of excitement churning within her.

'OK—I'm listening,' he replied, gathering up the drawings and rising to his feet. He placed the work on the desktop, a gleam of challenge in the eyes that met hers. 'I believe you were filling me in as to the nobility of your nature compared with that of other mere mortals such as myself.'

'I'll have you know I had to scrimp and save to get my design qualifications,' she rounded on him hotly. 'My concern is as much for my own reputation as that of this company!'

He returned to the chair, flinging his long, lean body down on it, his eyes watchful and alert.

'One thing I do know about my sister is that she wouldn't have allowed herself what she considers the luxury of unscheduled leave unless she was certain it wouldn't affect her business in any way.' His eyes narrowed. 'And, scrimp and save though you may well have had to do, I was under the impression, that, no matter how good your qualifications, you were a recent recruit to Jennifer's team and were, therefore, serving what amounts to an apprenticeship—for want of a better word.'

'You don't have to bother trying to be diplomatic,' retorted Abby sharply, determined to give him no hint of her astonishment that he had. 'Of course I'm still very much learning the ropes here, though I could name several interior designers with years of experience who'd give anything to be in my shoes.'

'So what makes you feel your reputation—not to mention that of my sister—could be in jeopardy?'

'It's Lady Morrison,' sighed Abby. 'I don't know if the name means anything to you, but her husband, Sir Jack——'

'The shoe magnate—I know,' he interrupted impatiently. 'They've bought a place on Richmond Hill that they want doing up. I believe Jennifer's got Peter Simmonds on it.'

'That's right,' said Abby, thrown by his knowledge of a concern he claimed to know nothing of, especially his ability to name one of his sister's top colleagues. 'Unfortunately Peter was involved in what seemed to be a minor car accident just over a week ago. It wasn't until the day after, when he suddenly collapsed, that it was discovered he'd damaged his back.'

'How badly?' demanded Max, clearly concerned.

'His wife says there won't be any lasting effects, as long as he remains immobile for at least a couple of weeks.'

'The poor devil,' muttered Max. 'He'll not like that.'

Abby gave an involuntary smile—he obviously knew Peter well. 'No, he won't. And that's why they're keeping him in hospital for the necessary period.'

'And now this Morrison woman has started complaining,' exclaimed Max disgustedly.

'Bitterly,' agreed Abby. 'But not for the reasons you're probably thinking. Apart from having heard somewhere that Jennifer Bradley Designs is the tops, she knows little or nothing. I don't even think she realises that Peter's one of the top interior designers in the country, because——'

'I hate to interrupt,' he snapped, doing precisely that, 'but I can't see what your problem is. If everything's been planned and decided and the work started, surely you're capable of stepping in and seeing the thing through.'

'I'm perfectly capable of it,' retorted Abby hotly. 'And if you'd let me finish you'd have learned that when Peter took me along to meet her she appeared to have got it into her head that I was in overall charge, instead of just there to learn at his side. Needless to say, when I mentioned it he just laughed, but now, with him in hospital, her mistake is probably something of a blessing in disguise.'

'Do you ever actually arrive at any point you attempt to make?' he drawled in tones of weary boredom.

'The point is that Lady Morrison seems to think she's entitled to deviate from all the plans at will. Reminding her that, apart from everything else, specialist tradesmen and carefully chosen materials are already on site has little or no effect. I had her on the phone for the best part of an hour not long ago and got virtually nowhere.'

'Damn, damn, damn,' he chanted softly to himself, then dragged impatient fingers through his hair. 'The last thing I want is Jennifer getting wind of anything like this!'

'Max—what's wrong with her?' Abby blurted out before she had time to bite back the words.

'There's nothing wrong with her,' he exclaimed sharply, then virtually retracted that claim. 'It's just that she's run down and needs a thorough rest. She and her husband, Paul... but you know Paul, don't you?'

'No!' exclaimed Abby, thrown by the unexpectedness of the question. 'I... I might have seen him on the odd occasion he's called in here,' she stammered in an attempt to mitigate the vehemence with which she had denied knowledge of Paul Lawson, the man she had once regarded as her future brother-in-law and who had broken her sister's heart when he had left her for another woman. The discovery that that other woman was Jennifer Bradley, whose successful business she still conducted under her maiden name, had come to her only weeks ago, shattering the euphoria still gripping her over her dream job and filling her with a gnawing sense of betrayal of the sister she adored.

She had been thrown by Paul's reaction to seeing her that first time he had turned up at his wife's office, and had been thrown too by the uncompromising vehemence with which she had later spurned his every attempt to talk to her. But what she had never since been able to rid herself of was the untenable yet niggling suspicion that her unyielding rejection of Paul was in some way connected with Jennifer's suddenly strained attitude towards her—not to mention her unexplained absence relatively soon after. She had told herself time and again it was irrational in the extreme for her to make any such connection with either occurrence...but the doubts lingered on none the less.

'Anyway—as I was saying,' stated Max, his eyes narrowed and speculating as they held hers, 'I don't want any of this getting back to Jennifer.' He gave a resigned shrug of his shoulders as she returned his gaze with frowning uncertainty. 'I suppose I've no option but to admit you were right, that my being here isn't coincidental—well, not entirely. Paul and I had been trying for some time to talk Jennifer into taking a break and when an idiot friend of mine I let use my studio for a couple of hours managed to set it on fire we suggested she pack her bags and let me take over this place until mine had been sorted out.'

'So why on earth couldn't you admit you were in charge,' demanded Abby exasperatedly, 'instead of palming me off each time I tried to approach you?'

'I'm a cartoonist, for heaven's sake!' he exclaimed with acerbity. 'I wouldn't have the first idea how to run this place. It's Jennifer's office I've taken over, not her business. I sign the odd cheque in her stead, when required to, but that's as far as it goes. As I've said, Jennifer would never have agreed to taking time off unless she was certain everything would run like clockwork without her.' He broke off, frowning. 'I know the other designers are fully occupied with their own projects, but surely one of them could give you advice, if not assistance.'

Abby pulled a face. 'Naturally I've spoken to them all, but, as far as I can gather, the mere idea of a client having the temerity to try arguing with, let alone dictating to a Bradley designer is beyond their comprehension . . . It's probably all my fault,' she exclaimed miserably. 'Perhaps I should have been more assertive with Lady Morrison the first time she started any of this. After all, we'd never have got to this stage if she hadn't agreed all the plans in the first place.' She broke off with a shudder. 'Though heaven only knows how she brought herself to agree to Peter's plan—she has the most appalling taste. No interior designers in their right minds would want their name associated with any of the schemes she's been suggesting to me over the past few days—especially not someone of Jennifer's faultless reputation.'

'If that's the case, it looks as though I'll have to join your team and see if together we can do something to straighten out this troublesome lady,' announced Max, rising to his feet and stretching.

'You?' croaked Abby in disbelief.

'Yes—me,' he replied with a disarmingly mischievous grin. 'Who else is there?'

'But you've already admitted you know nothing about interior design.'

'Granted, but I'm exceptionally skilled at getting my own way,' he replied, the lazy sweep of his eyes up her body bringing the hot sting of colour to her cheeks. 'In fact, I can't think of a time when I've really put my mind to it that I haven't ended up getting my own way.'

'Well, I wouldn't bet on it with Lady Morrison if I were you,' said Abby, irritated by the tenseness in her voice that betrayed her reaction to his deliberate goading.

'But what about you, Abby?' he asked, taking a stride towards her. 'Would you bet on the odds of my getting my way with you?'

'Life's just one big joke as far as you're concerned, isn't it?' Cornered, she was lashing out blindly at him, her only defence attack. 'You don't give a damn about your sister; in fact, you don't seem to give a damn about anything just so long as you can have your fun!'

'Let's get one thing straight, shall we?' he said, his words soft with threat. 'I have as many faults as the next man, though I dare say there are plenty enough women around prepared to swear I have more—but, make no mistake, I love my sister, and God help anyone who does anything to hurt her while I still have breath in my body!'

'I'm certain Lady Morrison has no intention whatever of hurting anyone,' exclaimed Abby, startled and feeling inexplicably threatened by the vehemence of his outburst. 'It's just that she's not particularly bright.'

He flashed her a look that did nothing to reassure her with its wary suspicion.

'To hell with Lady Morrison!' he snapped. 'From what you've said all she needs is a bit of firm handling.'

'I only hope you're right,' muttered Abby, her inexplicable feelings of edgy uncertainty spilling over into her words.

'Just you wait and see,' he chuckled, his unexpected laughter so distracting her that she scarcely noticed his hands reach out to hers.

She noticed them with a vengeance the instant they covered her own, his fingers exerting no discernible pressure as they lightly encircled her wrists.

'Now—to get back to these odds on my getting my wicked way with you,' he murmured with taunting softness.

'At least you're prepared to admit it would be wicked,' retorted Abby in what she knew to be a feeble attempt to joke her way out of a situation she hadn't the least idea how to extract herself from.

The instant he had taken her hands in his she had wisely resisted the temptation of trying to free herself, accepting that her strength would be only a fraction of his.

'Let go of me,' she demanded, her tone remarkably controlled given that the gentle, stroking movements of his thumbs against her skin was sending her pulses racing. And it wasn't just her pulses, she thought in weak disbelief; there was also this devastatingly melting softness slinking its way through her, stirring up a restlessness of longing in her that she could put no name to and trapping her breath like a pain in her lungs.

'I've got you at something of a disadvantage, Abby,' he taunted.

'Haven't you just!' she exploded, the trapped air escaping raggedly from her. 'You're twice my size and——'

'And I've my fingers on your pulses,' he finished for her with a soft laugh. 'It's strange—from the first moment I looked into those bewitching green eyes of yours I began fantasising about affecting you just like this.'

'If you mean making me boil with rage, your fantasies have come true!'

'Boil, yes—but not with rage,' he murmured complacently and then, making no attempt to draw her to him, leaned over and kissed her briefly, full on the lips.

He was laughing softly to himself as he drew back from her, leaving her in no doubt that he had somehow discerned the searing need that had flashed through her for that kiss to continue.

Furious with herself, she rounded on him. 'If you have any ideas of my handing myself to you on a plate as some sort of a reward for helping me out with Lady Morrison—not that I'm in the least convinced you can anyway—forget it! I'd rather give up my job!'

He released her hands instantly, an expression of scowling anger darkening his handsome face.

'What a peculiarly twisted little mind you have,' he rasped. 'And how incredibly naïve you appear to be.'

He hauled her into his arms, his lips crushing down on hers in bruising anger.

Unable to hit out at him with the fists trapped against his chest, Abby's body began twisting in violent protest against his. It was the effect of those frenzied movements on the lean, taut body against which she was trapped that took them both unawares and halted any vestige of combat between them. There was the soft groan of passion rumbling at the back of his throat as hot urgency replaced the punishing anger of the mouth plundering hers and his arms slid possessively around the body now moulding itself in trembling acquiescence to the vibrant heat of his.

'Damn it, Abby!' he groaned, tearing himself free from her now clinging arms. 'Do you require any further proof that neither of us needs to resort to blackmail to hand themselves on a plate to the other?'

Already convinced she was about to collapse from the force of the sensations still blasting their way throughout her, Abby had to grip the desktop in order to find the strength to accommodate the relief now flooding through her at his virtual admission that he had been similarly affected. Her eyes rose to his, the words that would unequivocally voice her relief already forming on her lips—only to die unuttered as their eyes met.

The desire was undoubtedly still there, but it was a naked rawness, a glittering fury of desire that scorned its own very existence.

'You can have me on a plate, Abby,' he informed her with hoarse venom. 'But can you handle knowing that you'll want me as you've wanted no other man... and that you get me only on a temporary basis?'

CHAPTER TWO

ABBY pottered her way through breakfast the following Monday morning, her thoughts, far from dwelling on the week ahead, drifting back over past years.

She and her sister Elaine had been fifteen and eighteen respectively when their lives had been shattered by the death of both their parents. One moment they had been cocooned in the warmth of an exceptionally close and loving family, the next their carefree world had been destroyed by the criminally careless actions of a man too befuddled by drink to be capable of controlling the car he drove down a winding country lane late one balmy summer's evening. The head-on collision resulting from that drunken spree left a once joyfully whole family halved and two teenage girls devastated by a grief so terrible their minds had difficulty containing it.

There had been a time when neither of them could envisage that lacerating harshness of acceptance ever leaving them, she remembered with a searing shiver of pain—but time had done its promised job. Just as there had later been a time when she had thought Elaine would never recover from the devastation of Paul's desertion, she reminded herself bitterly. But it had taken a successful career move on Elaine's part, together with time, before those particular wounds had begun to heal. Was it really four years since all that turmoil? she wondered almost disbelievingly. She had been nineteen at the time and near to completing the foundation course that was to be her entry to her degree course in interior design.

Yet even now she could remember vividly that morning the letter had arrived from their uncle Mick, their mother's brother, the principal of a school in Vancouver for physically handicapped children, offering Elaine a job there. Almost as though to distract herself from the memory of how her heart had sunk those years ago, she glanced at her watch and decided she had time for another cup of tea before leaving.

The job their uncle had offered Elaine was one right after the heart of a girl who adored children and had endless patience with them, not to mention a glowing record as a primary school teacher. Sipping her tea, Abby relived the feelings that had then assailed her as Elaine had read out their uncle's letter. There had been that stifling sensation of imminent abandonment coupled with the sudden and guilty realisation that, had it not been for her feelings of responsibility towards her younger sister, Elaine would most certainly have looked far further afield than the local primary school at which she had taught ever since qualifying.

She finished her tea, thankful that, despite having been very young for her nineteen years, she had somehow found the strength to mask her own fears and urge Elaine to accept their uncle's offer.

She rose, at last forced to face up to the fact that she was killing time, dithering around while pandering to a positive reluctance to embark on the day ahead. She glanced out of the kitchen window of the comfortable maisonette overlooking the Thames in Kingston into which she and Elaine had moved shortly after their parents' death, frowning at the sight of the hazy, late September drizzle greeting her. It was at times like these that she desperately missed Elaine, she thought dejectedly, then pulled herself up sharply by enquiring of herself precisely what it was about this particular time that made it so different from any other. It didn't take her much soul-searching to come up with an answer—she had managed to get herself into something of a state, and the cause was the man she was due to meet in Richmond in twenty minutes.

Less than fifteen minutes later she pulled up in front of a porticoed mansion set back among a cluster of tall trees high on Richmond Hill and gave a cheery wave in response to a shouted greeting from one of the plasterers carrying materials from a van into the house.

There were two other vehicles in the semi-circular drive besides the little blue Renault she had inherited from Elaine, but no sign of the opulent silver Rolls-Royce Lady Morrison usually appeared in, nor of any car that might belong to Max.

Though normally she would have gone in and had a word, and perhaps a cup of tea, with the workmen, this time she sat tight in her car, lost in introspective thought and not in the least at peace with herself. It was a state of mind so alien and disturbing to her that she had spent the entire weekend mentally ducking and weaving in order to avoid even the slightest acknowledgement of its existence. Frowning with exasperation at her own ostrich-like stupidity, she began giving those ruthlessly suppressed thoughts their freedom.

When she and Max had made arrangements on Friday for this morning's meeting, the air between them had been charged with an almost palpable hostility. The truth was that while Max undoubtedly found her physically attractive he didn't actually like her—an idea that disturbed her so much she had spent an entire weekend blocking it from her mind. So...what about her feelings for him?

She had, of course, heard of him long before she had ever come to work for his sister—not that even then had she thought to link the cartoonist with the divine looks, renowned for the savagely incisive wit that leapt remorselessly from his work, with her new employer, despite their shared surname. But she had recognised him instantly that first time he had breezed into the office and sent every female heart within sight a-flutter.

'Look at them,' Jennifer had half groaned, half laughed from beside her. 'Whatever it is that wretched brother of mine has, I've yet to meet a woman who can resist it.'

Yet there had been an underlying pride, too, in her voice, Abby remembered...but that had been in the days when Jennifer had been friendly and relaxed in her company.

She gave a small shiver of apprehension as she faced the fact that, whatever it was Max had, she too had been inexorably drawn to it. And there was apprehension in the grim set of her delicately lovely features as she remembered the turmoil of that first kiss. She had no idea how she might have reacted had any other man managed to awaken that hitherto undreamed of core of raw sexuality within her—but that wasn't really what troubled her, she thought confusedly. There had been something else, something so elusive and which had touched her so fleetingly that all her memory could resurrect of it was a discomfiting sense of foreboding.

So lost had she become in the brooding bemusement of her thoughts that she was deaf to the soft purr of the powerful car drawing up behind her, as she was too to the barely detectable opening and closing of one of its doors.

She only just managed to choke back a shriek of fright when the door beside her of her own car was suddenly wrenched open.

'What, sleeping on the job already? My, that must have been some weekend!'

'Very amusing,' muttered Abby, climbing out. 'You're late,' she pointed out sharply.

She glanced up at the man now closing the door of her car, her eyes widening in bemusement—he was actually smiling. But as her glance took in what he was wearing, it was disbelief that caused her eyes to widen even further. One of the first things she had noticed about him was that he invariably dressed well, with that casually understated elegance that denoted faultless taste and the money to indulge it rather than any particular interest in clothes as such. But the gleaming, hand-stitched boots beneath immaculately tailored trousers, the baggy suede jacket of almost chamois softness, over one shoulder of which was slung the type of pale, light-weight raincoat that usually cost a small fortune—none of these came close to what would usually be worn around a place which, in areas, was virtually a building site.

'For heaven's sake, Max, you can't come here dressed like that!' she exclaimed exasperatedly.

'I hadn't realised this was a white-tie affair,' he murmured, his eyes lazily skimming her navy hooded anorak, paint-spattered jeans and equally scruffy trainers.

'Don't say I didn't warn you if you end up splattered with plaster and heaven only knows what else,' she muttered, turning on her heel and walking towards the huge open front door.

'I hate to disappoint you, sweetie,' he announced as he caught up with her, 'but I've no intention of mucking in around here—I'm only here to sweet-talk Lady M into submission, remember?'

It was on the tip of Abby's tongue to inform him she was not his or anybody else's 'sweetie', but she held it back—the mood he was in was a good deal better than anything she might have expected, in fact, so much better that she was beginning to wonder exactly what it was that had convinced her of his animosity towards her.

'Well, while you're busy doing all that sweet-talking, you'd still be well advised to watch where you're stepping and what you're brushing up against,' she muttered, her clipped words, she felt sure, betraying her underlying sense of unease.

'It appears you don't envisage having any problems over this,' declared Max with unmistakable challenge, pushing the heavy front door further open as they reached it.

'Over what?' asked Abby, stepping in past him and cursing the fact that she hadn't had the sense to stand up firmly to Lady Morrison right from the start. Had she done so, she reminded herself disgruntledly, she wouldn't have ended up in this ghastly position of having to pin her hopes on someone as unpredictable as Max to bail her out. Not only did he openly admit to knowing nothing whatever about the subject, but the way he seemed to regard the whole thing as something of a joke was beginning to make her feel very on edge.

'Over my chatting up another woman right under your nose,' he replied with mocking innocence. 'I really do hope I can trust you, Abby. We can't have you undoing all the good I do by baring your teeth and loosing off green-eyed daggers at poor old Lady M, can we?'

'Our client happens to be neither old nor poor,' responded Abby witheringly. Amanda—Lady Morrison—

was, in fact, a tall, statuesque and strikingly attractive blonde in her mid thirties, of whom several of the tabloids had unkindly hinted that it was her sixty-year-old husband's fortune, rather than his other attributes, which had captivated her. 'And before she arrives... Oh, heck!' Abby spun round towards the door. 'I've left all the copies of the room layouts in my car. I realise they'll probably mean little or nothing to you, but I'd planned taking you through them anyway before she arrives—that way you might not end up sounding a complete ignoramus should she happen to question you.'

He halted her in her tracks by grabbing hold of the hood of her anorak.

'Perhaps the fact that I've already studied the relevant plans, and also my happening to be blessed with a photographic memory, will ensure I come over as no more than a partial ignoramus should the lady concerned decide to quiz me,' he drawled.

Abby gave a non-committal shrug, then led them through the vast hall and on down to the rear of the ground floor to the completed kitchen and utility areas.

'I see your troublesome client hasn't done any interfering here,' remarked Max from behind her as she began checking that the one or two minor adjustments she had asked for had been attended to in the installation of the lavish equipment. 'This all seems to be exactly according to the plans... An indication that she's not the domesticated type, perhaps?'

He certainly seemed to have digested the plans pretty thoroughly, admitted Abby to herself, more than a little surprised.

'Actually, there are several areas in the house where she's left well alone—all of which are near completion,' she told him. 'The rooms proving such a headache are the main drawing-room, the formal dining-room and the remaining three bedrooms. The trouble is——'

'Abby—so this is where you're hiding!'

Both Abby and Max swung round. Amanda Morrison was silhouetted in the doorway, dressed in soft leather cowboy boots, designer jeans and a striking multi-coloured sweater; her long blonde hair was swept up high on her head and she looked altogether stunning.

'Now that the plasterers have finished... Good heavens, it isn't!' The cornflower-blue eyes that had travelled with such appreciation up the length of the strange male adorning her new kitchen widened in startled disbelief as they finally alighted on Max Bradley's handsome features. 'Bradley! You know, it simply didn't occur to me!' exclaimed Amanda Morrison, almost a dance in her step as she approached the man regarding her from narrowed eyes, an almost mocking half-smile on his lips. 'You must be Jennifer's brother-in-law!'

'I'm her brother,' stated Max laconically, while Abby gave him a surreptitious glance to find out what his reaction was to 'poor old Lady Morrison'. Whatever it was, his expression was giving nothing away, she thought, then decided a trifle waspishly that attractive women practically dancing with delight at the mere sight of him was something he regarded as rather boringly commonplace.

'But I thought Jennifer was married.'

'She is,' replied Max. 'She just happens to use her maiden name for her business.'

'Well, fancy her being the sister of the famous Max Bradley!' gushed the blonde, then clapped her hands together in glee. 'What a fantastic conversation opener it would be to have a Max Bradley cartoon as a mural in a dining-room!'

Abby froze in horror, while Max gave a slightly forced laugh.

'I don't know about a conversation opener,' he said. 'I'm afraid you'd be more likely to find any of my works stopping conversation stone-dead, not to mention killing off any appetite your poor guests might have started out with.'

Abby watched in fascination as her client valiantly strove to recover from such cavalier rejection of her idea, then moments later found herself almost open-mouthed with admiration at the skill with which she observed her unpredictable sidekick convince the unsuspecting woman that not only had he taken her remark as an intended joke, but also that it was one he considered remarkably witty.

'Something tells me that you're just the man I need right now, Max—you don't mind me calling you Max, do you?' she said, linking her arm conspiratorially through his and smiling up at him with total confidence. 'I hate formality, so you must call me Amanda—the way just about everyone around here does, don't they, Abby?'

Abby did her best to keep her face suitably composed; neither she nor, as far as she knew, any other member of the team had been invited to address their client by anything other than her title.

'Now, where was I? Oh, yes...you see, my Jack's away on business and he's expecting to come back and find this place ready for us to move into. It's got to the stage where I feel I need a bit of down-to-earth masculine guidance to help me make up my mind about the final touches here.'

Final touches, thought Abby weakly—what Amanda Morrison had in mind constituted major reconstruction!

'Despite having so talented a sister, I'm afraid I know next to nothing about this sort of thing,' replied Max, to Abby's complete horror. 'In fact, I'm just one of those men who knows what he likes and says so... though I've a feeling that's exactly the sort of woman you are, Amanda.'

'That's me to a T,' replied Amanda, her almost purring words accompanied by the most dazzling of smiles. 'I realise how terribly busy you must be... but I'd be so grateful if you'd give me your advice on the dining-room.'

'I'm sure I could find the time,' murmured Max, flashing Abby a wickedly gloating look as, with Amanda hanging like a limpet on to his arm, he moved towards the door. 'But I'm sure you've already guessed that I didn't just happen to drop by here,' he added in tones that immediately had Abby tensing with suspicion.

'So—what did bring you here?' asked Amanda, girlish laughter tripping through her words.

'To be honest, I wanted to see what Jennifer's lot were doing with this place,' he murmured with blatant dishonesty. 'I've a friend who's bought a similar property in London and he hasn't yet made up his mind what to do with it—perhaps you know of him.'

Abby rolled her eyes heavenwards as she heard him shamelessly drop the name of a distinguished actor, while Amanda positively squirmed with delight.

'Perhaps Abby should come along and take a few notes,' suggested Max, flashing her a disconcertingly evil smile over his shoulder as he and Amanda disappeared through the doorway.

Silently willing herself to hang on to what was left of her control, Abby fished deep in the pockets of her anorak and produced a notepad and pen. She had only herself to blame for this, she berated herself furiously. Her every instinct had warned her not to trust him, that expecting any sort of help from him would be little more than clutching at straws. But she had ignored her every instinct and now she was left with this horrible feeling that she had somehow walked into a trap. For whatever his reasons, there were moments when he undeniably felt animosity towards her, she reminded herself, panic now threatening to run riot in her, and now she had placed herself completely at the mercy of a sense of humour which she strongly suspected would turn out to be decidedly warped.

'Something tells me that you and my Jack will get on like a house on fire.'

Abby, who had spent the best part of three hours perched on a window ledge at the far end of the huge, virtually gutted room, her horror and disgust mounting as she strove not to listen to the flirtatious, innuendo-laden exchanges of her two companions, nearly fell off the sill in disbelief at the sound of Amanda Morrison's laughing statement.

How could any woman—especially one who had spent the best part of the morning issuing blatant invitations in every conceivable way, bar words, to a man who hadn't lifted so much as an eyebrow in any attempt to deter her—have the gall to introduce her husband's name in such nefarious circumstances? And there had been no hint of shame in her words!

'I do believe you could be right,' came Max's laughing words floating to her ears.

Abby closed her eyes, wanting to block out everything that was going on around her. To think that she had actually found him attractive, she fretted bitterly, cringing from the soft sound of their banter still filtering through to her. Well, at least the past few hours had put paid to anything she might have felt towards him, she told herself with a twinge of relief. He was a typical case of beauty being no more than skin-deep; beneath that stunning surface lay an unprincipled predator, a man who plainly had no qualms about poaching on another man's territory.

'Be with you in a minute, Abby,' Max called out to her.

'And I'll see you same time tomorrow,' added Amanda, giving her a cheery wave as she and Max disappeared from the room.

Hugging her arms around her, she leaned her head against the coldness of the glass, trying desperately to steer her mind away from any acknowledgement of the bitter hurt and disappointment gnawing away inside her. She had far more important things to occupy her mind than Max Bradley and his dissolute ways, she informed herself savagely—such as the complete hash she was managing to make of what should have been a perfectly straightforward overseeing job. But with Peter in hospital, Jennifer away and the rest of the senior partners dotted about the country on various assignments, there was no one of any authority with whom she could sit down and discuss the fact that she probably had no alternative but to hand in her notice.

'Come along, let's grab ourselves some lunch and you can fill me in on the next steps,' said Max, striding back into the room and over to her.

'The only next step I envisage is handing in my notice,' retorted Abby, the words bursting from her with the recklessness of an uncontrollable anger.

'What the hell's got into you?' he demanded, genuine amazement in his tone.

'Why should I try explaining to you? You're the last person who would understand—you regard everything as one colossal joke!'

'Which no doubt accounts for my success in my chosen profession,' he drawled coldly. 'But try me anyway.'

She flung up her hands in a gesture of complete despair. 'I simply haven't the experience to handle anything like this! You claim to be protecting Jennifer by not letting her know what's going on. She left assuming that, apart from it being all cut and dried, Peter was running this job. She'd have forty fits if she realised the way things actually are!'

'Don't be so melodramatic. Anyone would think Amanda was—— '

'I know what Amanda Morrison is—she's trouble whichever way you care to look at it!' exploded Abby. 'If she doesn't get her own way, she'll pull out and make a song and dance about doing so—if she does get her own way and some of her ghastly ideas end up being incorporated here, Jennifer Bradley designs might just as well say goodbye to their professional reputation!'

'If you've quite finished,' he intoned with exaggerated patience, 'I'd——'

'No—I haven't finished! For a start I'm wondering why I give a jot about this company's reputation—no one here seems to have any idea about team spirit!' she raged, her pent-up grievances now flowing from her fast and furious. 'I've approached everyone I possibly can, but it's as though none of them gives a damn. They look at me with an air of disbelief, then mutter vaguely about how confident they are I'll sort whatever it is out. I'm a raw recruit straight out of art school, for heaven's sake!'

'And what makes you think that they're not fully aware of that fact?' enquired Max, his tone cold and impersonal. 'Correct me if I'm wrong, but wasn't it Jennifer and most of these people you're now complaining about who formed the panel that interviewed you and subsequently offered you this job?'

'Yes, but——'

'No buts, Abby,' he warned, all impersonality gone as he reached forward and hauled her to her feet, anger glinting in his eyes, 'just a few facts. Now—I may know nothing about interior design, but one thing I'm certain of is that you wouldn't have got so much as a foot through the door of a company with the professional reputation my sister enjoys unless she and her colleagues were one hundred per cent certain you were worth taking on. Who knows? Perhaps they were so blinded by your artistic skills that they didn't spot the chicken-hearted streak in you that——'

'How dare you?' she howled.

'I'll tell you how I dare!' he roared back, gripping her by the shoulders and forcing her to face him as she tried to turn from him. 'All I hear from you is your whingeing about ruined reputations, about Amanda's ghastly taste and about there being no one for poor little Abby to run to for help! Damn it, Abby, there's no problem there for you to be running to anyone with. What there is is a minor spot of bother, mainly of your own making. Do you honestly believe Amanda's mercurial mind-changes only began manifesting themselves the other day? Of course they didn't, but a watertight contract was, nevertheless, eventually thrashed out with the Morrisons. And if you believe that Amanda mistook you for the boss instead of Peter, you'll swallow anything!'

'But Peter——'

'I said no buts—remember, Abby?' he cut in harshly. 'Of course Peter knew damned well she'd made no such mistake—he was probably only too happy to have her off his back. But even knowing what tricks Amanda might try pulling on you, I'm certain Peter's not lying in his hospital bed fretting over how you're coping. Like the rest of them, he respects your talents and assumes you'll just be getting on with the job.'

'And all I've done is let him and everyone else down,' whispered Abby defeatedly, unable to disagree with a single word he had uttered. 'You may find this hard to believe, but nobody could ever have wanted a job as much as I wanted this one with Jennifer. And when I had to step in for Peter, I was so determined to do well...yet the moment I was faced with a problem...instead of standing back and looking at it logically I just panicked,' she stammered hoarsely. 'And now I've made a complete hash of everything.'

'Where's the hash?' he asked, his tone softening. 'OK, so you panicked and mishandled Amanda, when all you had to do was refer her to the contract—but Amanda's no longer your problem.'

'No longer my problem?' she gasped, wrenching herself free as anger flared hotly in her. 'Why—because you've taken her over? How conceited can you get? Just because the pair of you spent the morning practically devouring one another doesn't alter the problem I have with her one iota!'

'And what exactly is your problem with her, Abby?' he asked with chilling softness. 'Don't tell me your jealousy's already getting the better of you?'

'Don't flatter yourself,' she flung at him, her eyes bright with scornful indignation as they met his. 'Perhaps scores of women are initially attracted by your looks, but I'm sure most of them feel nothing but disgust once they discover your morals are little better than that of an alley cat.'

'No doubt other women would; but not you, Abby,' he said, his laughter harsh and humourless as he caught her by the upper arms and almost lifted her against him. 'Perhaps it's because you regard us as two of a kind that you find me so overwhelmingly irresistible?'

'I don't... I don't find you anything of the sort,' she stammered, her words barely coherent.

She was experiencing an overpowering sensation of something within him reaching out to her, a hot velvety darkness that enfolded and then lazily permeated her, at first draining her and then replenishing her with its own languid, sensuous softness until there was no part of her untouched by its heady, throbbing sweetness.

'How do you find me, Abby?' he demanded huskily, his mouth for an instant mirroring the sensuous sweetness melting within her as it found hers.

But that brief moment of sweetness deteriorated into an explosive urgency that trembled as though electrically charged through the fingers impatiently unzipping her anorak and shivered itself against her skin. Her arms had locked themselves around his neck even before his hands had begun negotiating their impatient way past her clothing and the involuntary cry of pleasure torn from her, as those seeking hands found and cupped her breasts with tantalising gentleness, was swallowed up and lost in the fevered intensity of their clinging mouths.

Her body was no longer hers to command; it now danced to taut, quivering life beneath the delicate, inflammatory urgings of his hands. Each teasing, tormenting touch seared itself like a brand against her flesh, burning through her with a pleasure so intense it was comparable to pain—and still her body demanded more.

She wanted so much more that the need within her became a restless, voracious hunger, moulding her body to his in a desperation close to anger, then clinging in a confusion of shock and pleasure as it encountered the full force of a need that threatened to eclipse her own.

Her reaction was one of wild elation, but through it was already filtering an awareness that was curiously almost detached that, for the first time in her twenty-three years, she was experiencing the full awakening of her own sexuality. Close on the heels of that realisation came the memory of their first kiss and a far less detached acknowledgement of what had rendered it unique.

'Max,' she whispered, hunger still trembling undisguised on the mouth she had so reluctantly torn from his. 'Max.'

Her arms were still around him, her body still moulded in quivering acquiescence to the vibrant heat of his. When his hands stilled against the turgid fullness of her still straining breasts, then lowered to rest lightly on the curve of her hips, it was her own involuntary gasp of protest that was the only sound to invade the laden silence between them.

'Max, I can't . . . I don't want to play games like this with you,' she said, her words sounding incongruously calm to ears deafened by the sounds of the inner turmoil still raging on unabated in her.

Though desire still gleamed in stormy darkness in his eyes, and for an instant his hands tensed rigidly against her hips, there was no discernible expression on his face as he released her and stepped back from her.

'It's a bit late in the day for either of us to attempt denying what exciting games they would be.'

Abby felt a silent scream of protest jar through her at the sound of those almost tauntingly detached words. There could be no denying the excitement...but what of the pain? Though she had refused to acknowledge it, that first kiss had warned her that this was a man she could all too easily love. They might euphemistically refer to 'games'—and that was all it would be to him—but what they were discussing was lovemaking, and in her heart of hearts she knew that the man to whom she gave her body would be the one to whom she also gave her heart.

'I...I'm not trying to deny anything,' she parried edgily. 'I just don't want to discuss it.'

'But it so happens that I do,' he replied, his eyes narrowed and cold as they surveyed her. 'Alley-cat morals or not, you want me, Abby...so what's holding you back? Or perhaps I should be asking you who?'

Abby had no idea what her outward reaction was to his words, but inwardly it was one of shocked incredulity. Despite her almost total lack of experience in such matters she knew without doubt that what had flared between them had been experienced with equal intensity by them both—yet now he seemed to be asking her if there was a man she felt deeply enough about to want to remain faithful. How could he possibly believe she could respond to him as she had while being virtually in love with another man?

'There's no one,' she informed him, the tense anger in her words directed almost entirely at herself for her foolishness in being unable to dissociate the physical act of love from love itself—a problem he had clearly never encountered.

'No one at all, Abby?' he mocked softly.

She hesitated, tempted in that brief instant to claim she was madly, deliriously in love.

'No one at all,' she replied icily. Why even bother resorting to lying? Amanda Morrison had a husband—a fact which hadn't deterred him in the least.

'Now that really does surprise me,' he murmured silkily. 'Though, on the other hand, perhaps it shouldn't. You're a very beautiful woman, Abby—I suspect you have a problem in that men fall in love with you by the drove.'

Her lips tightening with anger, Abby turned and gazed sightlessly out of the window. He suspected nothing of the sort, she told herself grimly. She considered herself not in the least given to false modesty and admitted she was attractive, perhaps even a little above averagely so, thanks to having her mother's intriguing green eyes and the vibrantly rich hair both she and Elaine had inherited from their Grantham grandmother. But only on rare occasions had she ever felt truly beautiful, and probably more from an inner glow of happiness than from any true reflection of reality.

'Your concept of love and mine obviously differ drastically,' she informed him with stilted frigidity.

'Interesting,' he mused, as though deeply intrigued. 'What odds would you give on one person deliberately setting out to make another fall in love with him . . . or her—and succeeding?'

Abby spun round with an angry exclamation of impatience. 'You might have time to waste,' she rasped, striding determinedly past him. 'I happen to have work to get on with.'

'Are you telling me I'd be wasting my time if I were to try making you fall in love with me?' he called after her in mock indignation.

'Not only do I not like wasting my time, I also don't waste my breath by answering stupid questions!'

'If there's one thing I can't resist, it's a challenge as direct as the one you've just issued.'

'I haven't issued any...oh, forget it!'

Her cheeks flaming, she stormed from the room, her own shriek of fright drowning out the taunting laughter drifting out after her as she walked straight into a stack of decorating materials and went sprawling.

CHAPTER THREE

'ABBY, are you OK, love? I'll kill those idiots for leaving all that gear there!'

'I'm fine, Tony,' Abby reassured the anxious contractor helping her to her feet.

'Are you sure, love? Your legs must have taken an almighty whack on that stack of ladders.'

'I honestly am fine,' she managed, forcing a smile to her lips instead of releasing the bellow of pain trapped inside her—her shins, she was convinced, had been reduced to shattered fragments.

'What happened?' demanded Max, from somewhere behind her.

Leaving Tony to do the explaining, Abby began making her painful getaway; the last person she was up to facing, right now, was Max Bradley. She made her way slowly through the hallway and out to her car, amazed to discover that her legs, despite their multiple breaks, still had the power to keep her upright.

'And just where do you think you're off to?'

Her only thought to flee those hectoring tones, she lurched the last couple of steps forward to her car and leaned weakly against it. This was it—she had had enough!

'I've already told you—I've work to do. And besides, it's none of your business!'

'That's odd; I'm the one who kept telling you it was none of my business, remember?' he said, walking right up to her and gazing down at her half-slumped figure with an expression of mild irritation. 'But now that you've gone to all this trouble to convince me it is, don't try messing me about. I happen to have a considerable amount of my own work to get through, so whatever we do together will have to fit in around it—is that understood?'

'No, it isn't! And I...' She broke off in sudden panic—she was about to burst into tears...or be sick...or possibly even both!

As her mind became engrossed in a tortuous, though beneficially distracting examination of whether or not it actually was physically possible to do both at the same time, the fact that she was being hoisted up in strong arms barely registered with her. She had been carried some distance and already deposited on the passenger-seat of the car parked behind hers before anything much began registering with her. It was the softly opulent aroma of leather that first got through to her, then gradually the fact that she was sitting in a car, sideways on a dark green leather seat, her still agonisingly painful legs dangling out through the open door.

'Put your head on your knees for a few moments,' Max urged her, the light pressure of his hand against the back of her neck ensuring she obeyed.

She did so instantly, suddenly remembering the threat of tears and nausea that had gripped her and those few disconcertingly blank moments following it.

Only when she felt it was completely safe to raise her head did she do so—and immediately wished she hadn't.

With one arm resting across the hood of his car and the other along the rim of the open door, Max was stooped over and gazing down at her. His expression was one of pensive concentration but, as so often, it was his eyes that seemed to offer reflection of his inner self and it was an indefinable something that she glimpsed in their darkly brooding depths that sent a shiver of apprehension down her spine.

'Do you feel better?' he asked, his expression blanking to one of polite concern, then, before she had a chance to reply, added, 'You went as white as a sheet—I thought you were going to pass out.'

'I . . . I feel much better now. Thanks.'

Her mind was still struggling to recapture exactly what it was she had glimpsed in his eyes, but with no success. Whatever it had been, she had probably over-reacted to it; she wasn't exactly feeling her best right now, she told herself, then wondered, with a feeling of slightly limp detachment, why it was that he appeared to be getting down on his knees before her.

'What on earth are you doing?' she asked in bemusement as, crouched, rather than kneeling, he began easing her jeans up one of her legs.

'Inspecting the damage—hell, no wonder you all but passed out on me!'

Forced to discard the idea that he was about to prostrate himself and apologise for the look he had given her, Abby gazed down at the trickle of blood oozing from the livid bruising revealed on her shin.

'You roll up the other one,' he instructed, leaning into the car and opening the glove compartment. 'I'm sure there's a first-aid box somewhere in here.'

Suffocatingly conscious of the body wedged against hers as he still searched, Abby began rolling up the other leg of her jeans. She glanced dismissively at the bruising on the shin that not so long before she had felt bone must be protruding from and wearily closed her eyes.

All right, so she had taken a nasty tumble, she told herself uneasily, and she was very likely suffering some measure of shock as a result. But that had no bearing whatever on the way she was reacting to this man—a way that could well prove disastrous for her!

'Here we are!' he exclaimed, reaching an arm across her and grasping the seat back for balance as he began easing his torso from the car.

Abby automatically turned to facilitate him and found her face unnervingly close to his and her pulses pounding out of control. She wasn't sure if it was her heart or her stomach twisting itself into tight knots of almost terrorised excitement—perhaps it was both—but, had she had any doubts that the sharp inhalation of breath from the man beside her was an indication that his reaction had been as equally involuntary and highly charged as her own, the naked need that flamed momentarily in the smoky blue of his eyes would have instantly obliterated them.

'So...we'd best see what we have here,' he muttered hoarsely, easing himself fully from the car and returning to his crouched position before her.

Incapable of coherent thought, let alone speech, Abby dropped her gaze to the dark head beside her, which was now bent in concentration on the contents of the first-aid box. She felt her fingers flex on her lap, actively resisting a compulsive urge to reach out and touch the hair showing a half-hearted tendency towards curling under its fine sheen of rain.

This wasn't, couldn't be happening to her, she told herself weakly. But it was—an almost textbook case of infatuation and with a man who was a textbook recipient of such infatuations, a highly successful, sophisticated man of the world, and one who, unfortunately, also happened to possess the sort of looks that could stop traffic.

'I'm the first to admit that what little I know about medicine is probably lethal,' he muttered, frowning in deep concentration as he began smearing cream on a patch of lint.

'But you're obviously not about to let that deter you from treating me though,' said Abby, the involuntary note of almost humorous indulgence in her tone startling her and eliciting an equally startled look from him.

Then he smiled at her, a twinkling, teasing grin that tied up every part of her in constricting knots.

'Unfortunately this kit doesn't run to an anaesthetic, which rules out surgery—so all I can offer is a dab of antiseptic cream where the skin's broken.' As he spoke he gently placed the lint over her cut shin and then bandaged it neatly in place. 'And now I prescribe lunch,' he announced, lowering her jeans leg back into place.

'If you say so, Doctor,' she quipped, her voice not altogether steady.

'I do say so—I'm hungry,' he chuckled, rising. 'Though lord knows where we'll find a decent eating place willing to accept you in that get-up,' he added before walking round to the other side of the car and getting in.

Abby pulled a small face as she eased herself properly into the car, but her thoughts didn't linger for long on her scruffy attire. There was, she suspected, a good deal more to Max than his status and good looks, she was admitting to herself as the engine purred to life, such as that unsuspected kindness that had manifested itself so spontaneously in him concerning her injuries.

'What about my car?' she exclaimed as they swept past it, almost grateful to have something to say that might distract her from her increasingly discomfiting thoughts.

'What about it?' he muttered. 'If you don't think you'll feel up to driving it after we've eaten, I can always arrange for someone to fetch it for you.'

'I'm sure that won't be necessary,' she said; then, desperate to keep conversation flowing, added, 'What's this car called?'

'Odd though it may seem, I haven't actually got around to giving it a name,' he drawled in reply. 'What's yours called?'

'I meant what make is it?' she retorted stiltedly, while an imp in her wondered how he would have reacted if she had simply replied 'Reggie'—the name she and her sister had christened the car the day Elaine had bought it.

'It's an Aston Martin.'

She said nothing, but one surreptitious glance around her sleekly opulent surroundings brought it home to her that Reggie's price probably wouldn't even have covered the cost of the upholstery adorning this fortune on wheels.

By the time they were seated in the restaurant of his choice, the atmosphere between them had deteriorated to an extent that infatuation and the idea of his possessing good points were the furthest thoughts from her mind.

Despite her vociferous protests, he had practically frog-marched her into a place that positively reeked of elitist refinement, not to mention downright snootiness, and whose po-faced staff, she felt certain, wouldn't have thought twice about showing her the door had it not been for the presence of her companion.

The relentless throbbing of her legs only exacerbating her general feelings of abject misery, she buried her nose in the exquisitely hand-written and, as she had instantly divined, horrifically expensive menu and discovered, to her complete surprise, that she was starving.

'I meant it when I said I've work of my own to attend to,' he stated abruptly when their first courses arrived. 'I've deadlines to meet, so we'll just have to fit in what we can around them.'

'Whatever you say, sweetie,' replied Abby in a drawling parody of his own voice.

'And what the hell's that supposed to mean?' he demanded icily.

'Whatever you want it to mean,' retorted Abby, suddenly feeling gloriously free. 'I've had a lousy morning, I'm cold, and my shins are killing me. I didn't want to come here in the first place, but now I am here I've discovered I'm hungry. You can drone on as much as you like about your deadlines and the rest of the world having to fit in with them—but, as I said, I'm hungry and I intend eating.'

'Fine, I'll drone, but you make damned sure you listen,' he retorted. 'And just for the record, it's only you who's required to fit in with my work schedule.'

She could sense his eyes drilling into hers, but kept her own trained resolutely on her plate.

'Right, now that the Morrison dining-room's been dealt with——'

'What do you mean, "dealt with"?' demanded Abby, her eyes flying to his and encountering mocking amusement.

'I'd naturally assumed you were taking professional notes of every word I exchanged with Amanda this morning,' he murmured innocently. 'She's agreed to the original scheme in its entirety.'

'Its entirety?' croaked Abby.

'She's prepared not to deviate by so much as a single lick of paint,' he confirmed. 'And while I was at it, I had a word with the contractor who so gallantly scraped you off the floor after your tumble. He assures me he'll have his men working on it this afternoon.'

'And he will too,' exclaimed Abby, relief flooding her. 'Tony's brilliant at his job.'

'For one who's just announced she was here only for the food, you're doing rather a lot of talking, aren't you?'

'What about the rest of the rooms?' exclaimed Abby impatiently. 'Did she agree to those too?'

'My God, the exuberance of your gratitude overwhelms me,' he drawled. 'No, she hasn't agreed to the rest of them yet, but she will. One room at a time—that's the way to deal with Amanda.' He broke off, frowning, then added with exasperated censure, 'You really haven't the slightest idea how to handle people, have you, Abby?'

'And I suppose you do!' she exploded, her initial indignation swiftly blazing to anger. 'Tell me, is there any limit to the extent to which you're prepared to "handle" Sir Jack Morrison's wife in order to get this contract completed?'

'I do believe I detect a note of censure in your dulcet tones,' he drawled with biting sarcasm.

'Really?' retorted Abby. 'Well, it might come as something of a surprise to you to learn that women who practise on men the sort of tactics you advocate get called names that aren't in the least flattering!'

'And precisely what are these tactics you claim I'm advocating?' he enquired in tones that sent a shiver of apprehension through her even as they heightened her anger.

'I'm sure you don't need me to spell out what you were up to,' she replied with scorn. 'And you certainly wouldn't have used tactics like that on her husband.'

'You really have got problems if you think everyone can be handled in the same way,' he retorted, then added with a particularly humourless smile, 'And I would have hoped it went without saying that I'm not given to flirting with men.'

'But you're obviously not averse to doing so with their wives!'

For several seconds he watched her in silence, his expression derisive and taunting.

'What else would you expect of someone with the morals of an alley cat?' he eventually enquired. 'And you, Abby, you appear to be as pure as the driven snow. Perhaps that's what this apparently inexplicable attraction between us is all about—opposites, you being purity personified and me a total degenerate.'

The venomous undertones in his words unnerved her to such an extent that the appearance of two waiters, bearing the rest of their order, brought a visible start from her. This was crazy, she told herself incredulously; only a few weeks ago she had been on top of the world, and then everything had seemed to go wrong—now she was little better than a bag of nerves.

'It's just as well you have so little choice in the matter of our relationship,' he continued relentlessly once the waiters had left, 'because technically we should end up doing one another a lot of good. Once some of my degeneracy has rubbed off on you and some of your——'

'Shut up!' exploded Abby, flinging down her fork. 'Just stop baiting me and leave me alone!'

'Baiting you, Abby? What an odd thing to say,' he murmured, his tone mildly chiding. 'And one thing I hope I've made perfectly clear is that I've no intention of leaving you alone.'

'The only thing you've made clear is how warped your sense of humour is,' Abby flung at him, wondering how much more of this bizarre exchange she could possibly take.

'I wasn't attempting to be humorous—warped or otherwise,' he replied, with a nonchalance that only exacerbated her feelings of nervous tension. 'Tell me, Abby, what would you consider to be the normal course of events when boy meets girl and they're mutually attracted?'

Abby's initial look of surprise at the unexpectedness of such a question quickly turned to one of unmitigated suspicion, then she promptly began tucking into her food—she had no intention of taking part in whatever warped game he was now devising.

'Perhaps I should have mentioned that both protagonists are free agents,' he murmured helpfully.

Abby resolutely continued eating.

'Take your time answering, by all means,' he drawled, 'though it's hardly the poser of the century.'

Abby gritted her teeth in a futile attempt not to be goaded into rash retaliation.

'If that's the case, why don't you simply answer it for yourself?' she snapped.

He gave an irritated shrug. 'OK—I'd say that the normal response would be to let nature take its course. Though I put the question to you because you appear to hold other views.'

'Which, needless to say, make me abnormal!' exploded Abby, sickeningly aware of how close she was to losing her temper and furious for having allowed herself to be goaded into such a state. 'Well, you're entitled to your view, but so am I to mine and by no stretch of the imagination would any woman in her right mind equate you with the male half of any idyllic little boy-meets-girl scenario!'

'Why ever not?' he enquired with wide-eyed innocence.

Though her every instinct warned her to cut her losses and retreat before she ended up making a complete spectacle of herself, her pride refused to comply.

'Because your attitude towards women is precious little short of predatory,' she flung at him in fury. 'If you think I'd be foolish enough to risk letting nature take its course with a man who goes around stripping every woman in sight with his eyes, who can arrogantly announce to a woman that he intends trying to make her fall in love with him just for the heck of it and then accuses her of being abnormal when she——'

'Enough!' he protested, throwing up his hands in mock horror. 'To reply to your opening salvo, of course my attitude to women is fundamentally predatory, as is that of any other healthy, unattached male—not to mention a number of attached ones.'

'Fortunately there happen to be men around who don't subscribe to your prehistoric views,' retorted Abby scornfully.

'I was merely referring to the basics of the male psyche,' he replied, an expression of faint amusement on his handsome features as he tilted back his chair and perused her from narrowed eyes. 'Just because modern-day man doesn't go around clubbing women over the head and dragging them off to their lairs doesn't alter the fact that the fundamental instinct of every male is to chase the female.'

'And you, needless to say, hanker after the good old days.'

He righted his chair, his expression switching to one of disdain.

'Grow up, Abby,' he muttered. 'You seem to have got it into your head that I'm some sort of rapacious animal on the prowl, whereas all I'm doing is stating the obvious—that it's the male's natural instinct to chase the female. Corny as it may sound, I happen to have too much respect for women to try conning them into believing I'm something I'm not.'

'You snap your fingers and expect women to fall into your arms—and you've the nerve to call that respect?' squeaked Abby in outrage.

'I've never snapped my fingers at any woman,' he retorted coldly. 'I just happen to be a bit more open than some men when it comes to my sexual dealings with them.'

'Your sexual dealings with them?' exclaimed Abby scathingly.

'That is what we're discussing, isn't it?' he demanded derisively. 'The fact that we're sexually attracted to one another?'

It wasn't what they were discussing, Abby told herself angrily as the arrival of a waiter brought her much needed respite, it was what he was cold-bloodedly taunting her with.

'Would you like anything else?' he asked her.

Abby shook her head. 'Just coffee, thanks,' she added in as civil a tone as she could manage.

She watched him as he ordered coffee for them both, the bitter anger in her trying frantically to suppress the essential honesty in her that was unable to deny that much of what he had said about basic male instincts was valid.

'So—tell me, Abby,' he murmured, his eyes fixing her with a coolly impersonal gaze, 'why are you so hell-bent on fighting this attraction between us—or were you, perhaps, lying when you told me you were emotionally unattached?'

'I wasn't lying,' she protested, 'and I've already told you why I regard you as the last person any woman in her right mind would choose to become involved with.'

'No, Abby, you've hurled a few wild accusations at me, none of which has much in the way of foundation,' he contradicted her evenly. 'My main crime seems to be that I flirt. Hell, I do that with all and sundry if I'm in the mood—even my housekeeper and she, I would have you know, is a grandmother and most certainly doesn't regard me as having any evil designs on her.'

'And what about Amanda Morrison?' Abby blurted out before she could check herself.

'Precisely—what about Amanda?' he drawled, then frowned impatiently. 'Abby, why do I get the feeling you're not being in the least honest with me?' His eyes narrowed to cold slits. 'Let me guess—you're harbouring a guilty secret you're terrified I'll uncover should you let me get too close.'

'I...don't you think you're being a touch melodramatic?' she stammered, and could gladly have bitten off her own tongue as she felt colour blaze to her cheeks.

'If anything, I'd say I'd hit on something of a raw nerve,' he observed with almost clinical detachment.

And that was exactly what his jokingly barbed words had done, she acknowledged dazedly. She could think of few men she would less willingly love than Max Bradley...nor one she could more easily love despite her every instinct; and that was a secret she would guard whatever the cost.

'Would you like more coffee?' he asked once his watchful eyes had taken in every last detail of her speechless consternation.

Abby shook her head, noticing with relief that he was signalling for a waiter, and telling herself that relatively soon her ordeal would be over. Completely drained, it was as though the last shreds of her self-confidence were slipping from her and suddenly she felt desperately alone.

'Right, we'll go,' said Max, his words cutting through the bleakness of her thoughts.

She watched as he dealt with the bill, her thoughts turning with no prompting towards her sister. Right now she needed Elaine, she thought in desperation, her loving arms to hug her and her soothing voice to dispel this terrible sensation of no longer being certain who or what she was.

'Right—it's home for you and an afternoon of complete rest,' exclaimed Max, striding to her side and placing a supportive arm around her as her stiff and painful legs almost gave way beneath her when she rose. 'I'll arrange to have your car sent round to you later,' he informed her as he steered her from the restaurant and towards his car.

'How much later?' she asked numbly, her body's treacherous reaction to his nearness inflicting a far more acute pain on her than her injuries ever could. 'I have to get back to the office——'

'For heaven's sake, Abby, be reasonable!' he exclaimed impatiently. 'You can hardly walk, so how the hell can you even contemplate driving? In fact, it might be an idea to have a doctor examine you,' he added, helping her into the car.

'I don't need a doctor,' she protested once he had joined her. 'My legs just feel a bit stiff—I'll be all right once it's worn off.'

'Just so long as you put your feet up for the rest of the day,' he muttered. 'It's not as though there's anything more you can do regarding the Morrison place—so do the sensible thing and have the rest of the day off. By the way, where do you live?' he asked, starting up the car.

She told him and then spent the short journey huddled in the gloom of her plagued thoughts, the only glimmer of relief among which was the faintest of hopes that her tumble was in some way to blame for this ridiculous state she was in, but that soon her head would clear and she would return to normal.

'Don't forget to let me have your car keys,' he reminded her, holding the car door open for her and watching as she gingerly eased herself out.

She straightened up, then fished in her pockets for her keys, cursing in silent desperation when her trembling hands dropped the bunch she was trying to separate.

He lifted the bunch and deftly separated the house keys from those of the car.

'Come along,' he said, pocketing her car keys and taking her by the arm, 'let's get you inside.'

'I'm perfectly capable of walking to the front door unaided,' she muttered, wrenching free her arm.

Ignoring her ungracious words, he escorted her to the door and inserted the key in the lock.

'I'm sure you'll understand if I don't invite you in,' she stated stiffly as he returned the door keys to her.

'I understand completely,' he replied, placing his hands lightly on her shoulders. 'But you know, don't you, Abby, that it's impossible to put off the inevitable?'

'Your arrogance is positively breathtaking,' she hissed, her eyes refusing to meet his.

'Abby, there are times when I'm rightly accused of arrogance, but this isn't one of them.' He lowered his head till his lips were brushing lightly against hers, then drew back instantly as an almost perceptible charge surged between them. 'I want you, Abby,' he whispered huskily.

'How can you?' she blurted out, thoroughly disorientated by the electrifying effect that kiss, which hadn't even been a kiss, had had on her. 'You don't even like me!'

He jerked back from her, almost as though her words had been a physical attack on him.

'What on earth makes you say that?' he exclaimed, but it was his eyes that betrayed him, with their distinctly wary alertness.

'It's in your eyes,' she replied, no longer caring what she said as she leaned wearily against the door frame. 'There are times when they give you away.'

'Perhaps it's more a case of your imagination giving you away, Abby,' he said tonelessly. 'Perhaps there's something about you that you feel would make me dislike you were I to find it out.'

'We're back to my dark secret, are we?' she asked with weary indifference. 'Who knows, Max? Perhaps you're right.'

CHAPTER FOUR

'DARLING, I didn't get your letter till today. I don't know if I'd mentioned it, but Rob Freeland managed to get some of the kids on a two-week course at a specialist riding place near Montreal—Uncle Mick's hoping to get something similar going here.'

'That sounds wonderful,' said Abby, her spirits soaring at the sound of her sister's voice. 'Elaine, about that ghastly letter——'

'It was pretty ghastly, Abby,' cut in Elaine gently, 'but not for the reasons you're probably thinking. For all that I love it here, I really do miss being able to sit down and have a real heart-to-heart with you—you know how hard I find expressing myself in letters. I suppose that's one of the reasons I never got around to the subject of Paul.'

'Elaine, I didn't mean to——'

'Darling, let me have my say—otherwise I've a feeling we'll simply end up talking in circles,' interrupted Elaine pleadingly. 'Of course I was devastated when Paul broke off with me, but so much of what I felt towards him seems to have been linked up with my inability to cope with Mum's and Dad's death. Abby, I got involved with Paul at a time when I was emotionally incapable of handling any such relationship.'

'But he was just what you needed,' protested Abby, her mind balking at what she was hearing.

'No, he wasn't—not that anyone would have been able to persuade me of that at the time,' sighed Elaine. 'What

I actually needed was professional counselling and, quite frankly, it's only because Paul is such a decent and caring man that he was prepared to put up with what gradually became my almost obsessional attitude towards him. God, how trapped that poor man must have felt!'

'Trapped?' croaked Abby, scarcely able to believe her ears.

'Abby, his meeting and falling so deeply in love with Jennifer Bradley was the best thing that could have happened to us both in that we were forced to face up to reality.'

'Elaine, did you actually know her name?' asked Abby, her mind still having problems digesting her sister's words. 'I mean... before I got the job with her?'

'Yes, I did.'

'So when I first wrote and told you about the job...'

'Yes, love, I recognised the name immediately,' admitted Elaine, the hint of a chuckle in her voice astounding her already severely bemused sister. 'I actually sat down to write and tell you who she was, then I had second thoughts. Darling, it was your very first job and one you were obviously thrilled to bits about. I suppose I was being ridiculously overprotective, but I didn't want the least little thing making you feel in any way uncomfortable right then, so I decided to put off telling you for a while. Now I realise how stupid that was. Abby, I can't tell you how guilty I felt when I got your letter.' She groaned. 'I gave you no credit for being the intelligent adult you now are and in doing so I've obviously caused you no end of anguish.'

'Elaine, don't be so daft, I... heck, I honestly don't know what to say. I suppose I had visions of you eating your heart out for Paul for the rest of your life, even though I could tell how happy you were in Canada.'

'You can't begin to imagine how happy... Oh, Abby, I could kill myself for having put you through so much worry, and so unnecessarily!'

'You don't have to go that far, but even if you weren't such a lousy letter-writer you'd still be right about missing being able to sit down and chat—which is why I've already started saving so that I can visit you.' Except that saving would take an age, she thought disconsolately, and what she desperately needed was to be able to sit beside Elaine and talk her heart out right now.

'How about Christmas?' asked Elaine, her voice sounding ominously unsteady.

'Darling, I'll never have saved enough by then,' exclaimed Abby, upset by the distress in her sister's voice and trying desperately to sound light-hearted.

'That won't be necessary. Oh, heck, I'm doing this all wrong!' groaned Elaine. 'Abby, it's Rob who'll be paying your fare—so that you can be our bridesmaid on Boxing Day!'

'Rob?' squeaked Abby. 'The school's doctor?'

'Abby, I mentioned him often enough in my letters,' protested Elaine. 'But every time I tried writing to tell you how wonderful he was I... it sounded so schmaltzy I tore it up!'

'Elaine, what age is he, for heaven's sake?' exclaimed Abby.

'Thirty—why?'

'He is the paediatrician, isn't he?'

'Yes. Abby——'

'Elaine, I distinctly remember you writing and telling me the paediatrician was a lovely, silver-haired old man!'

'Abby, that was Robert Turner—he retired ages ago and Rob took over from him...oh, hell,' groaned Elaine. 'Robert and Rob!'

'Precisely, you idiot! From your letters it was perfectly plain you regard him as the greatest thing since sliced bread, but as I had no idea he was an eligible thirty-year-old you'll understand that I didn't even attempt reading between the lines!'

'Oh, Abby, I... I think it's best if I hand you over to Rob, while I go and bang my thick head against the wall a few times!'

'Hi, Abby,' laughed a soft, Canadian-accented voice down the line. 'It's Rob Freeland here, your soon-to-be brother-in-law.'

'Hello, Rob,' replied Abby with delight. 'I take it you realise I've been under the impression you were a silver-haired old gent.'

'You'll be able to check for yourself that I'm not, come Christmas,' chuckled Rob. 'I hope there won't be any problems for you getting here—the wedding of the year will be ruined if the chief bridesmaid doesn't show up.'

'Don't worry,' promised Abby, immediately warming to him, 'nothing could stop me. I'm so happy for you both.'

'Thanks, and it's great to be able to have a few words with you,' said Rob, his tone serious. 'I know how hard it is for you and Elaine having all these miles separating you, especially at a time like this, that's why I wanted to let you know that no harm will ever come to her while I'm around—I love her and I want nothing more than to be able to spend the rest of my life with her.'

The memory of that telephone call remained with her throughout the day, now and then rearing up in her with such warmly satisfying strength that it gradually made her question the quality of her own happiness when that of her sister could so completely preoccupy her.

Of course she was happy, she told herself irritably, pushing aside the plans she had been working on. Admittedly, for a while, things had been ghastly—but that was all behind her. Contrary to her gloomy expectations, and true to his boastful promises, Max had succeeded in getting the Morrison contract completed more or less to schedule...and also, thank heavens, he seemed to have lost interest in propositioning her in that aggressively sexual way he had initially. In fact, he seemed to have lost interest in her full stop, she admitted in an unguarded moment before the shutters of her mind descended, as they now invariably did, on any comprehensive examination of her feelings towards Max. Her job was going extremely well, she reminded herself doggedly. Since Peter's return she had been given one or two projects, albeit relatively minor ones, to run on her own and had carried them through with complete success.

'Come in,' she called, startled from her thoughts by a muffled thud on her office door. 'Julie, what on earth are you doing carrying weights like that around?' she exclaimed aghast, leaping to her feet and running to the assistance of the petite blonde office manageress staggering across the room beneath a mound of pattern books.

'Today just hasn't been my day,' groaned Julie, depositing the samples on the desk and collapsing on to the nearest chair. 'Freddie and half the clerical staff are off with flu and the switchboard's been out of commission for most of the day because of some emergency cable works.' She gave Abby an impish, though decidedly weary grin. 'The only thing likely to ward off my impending nervous breakdown is a good strong coffee.'

'Coffee coming up on the double,' promised Abby.

When she had first begun work she had had no idea what the role of an office manageress entailed, though she had quickly learned that it was this deceptively ethereal-looking girl who kept the nucleus of the company running with such apparently effortless efficiency.

'Peter said you'd promised to have a rummage through those for him,' Julie murmured, indicating the samples, her face brightening as Abby handed her a coffee.

'Yes, he mentioned them yesterday,' said Abby, returning to her seat with her own coffee. 'But you shouldn't have brought them up. I'd have come down if you'd given me a ring...' She broke off, pulling an apologetic face. 'Though I suppose you couldn't, because of the phones.'

'Precisely,' sighed Julie, then raised her cup. 'Cheers, I really needed this. As you can probably imagine, I've been flying around like a dervish most of the day—oh, before I forget, there's a staff meeting first thing tomorrow morning.'

Abby took a sip from her mug in an attempt to mask her surprise. The design teams normally had meetings on the last Friday afternoon of the month—so this one was decidedly out of the ordinary.

'Actually, it was Jennifer who came round to see me last night and asked me to set it up,' said Julie.

This time Abby was unable to hide her surprise.

'How is Jennifer?' she asked diffidently.

'She's fine,' replied Julie, then hesitated. 'In fact, she's on top of the world! I know you'll keep this to yourself till after tomorrow's meeting, but I just had to tell someone—she's pregnant!'

'How wonderful!' exclaimed Abby, then added anxiously, 'But there's nothing wrong, is there? I mean . . . she left work so suddenly.'

'Everything's fine,' Julie assured her. 'Poor Jennifer—she and Paul had been trying for a baby ever since they got married, but when it actually happened she ended up getting into a most un-Jennifer-like state about it. She felt pretty rough for the first couple of months and got paranoid about miscarrying, though there was absolutely no reason for her to.' She took a sip from her cup, then sighed. 'I suppose, not having known her very long, you wouldn't have noticed it, but Jennifer most definitely hadn't been her usual self before she left.'

She had noticed it all right, thought Abby, feeling as though an invisible weight had been removed from her shoulders.

'Anyway, she's called tomorrow's meeting to discuss her long-term plans,' said Julie, glancing at her watch, then rising. 'I wonder if they'll entail our having the divine Max as a . . . heavens, Max! Abby, did you get his message?'

Abby shook her head. She had neither seen nor heard from Max in the last couple of days—a fact which had, in many ways, rendered those days virtually stress-free.

'He rang just before the telephone engineer arrived,' groaned Julie. 'You weren't in your office, so I told Sally I'd pass on the message.'

'If it's about his drawings for the American magazine——'

'No—it's about you and him having dinner with the Morrisons tonight,' cut in Julie anxiously. 'He forgot to mention it the last time he saw you.'

Abby pulled a face. 'I wish you'd forgotten too.'

'It wouldn't have done you much good,' chuckled Julie, 'because the rest of his message was that he'd pick you up at eight.'

'But I might easily have had something else arranged,' protested Abby. 'What's so funny?' she demanded, as Julie burst out laughing.

'I never thought I'd see the day when I heard a woman react as you just have to the prospect of an evening in the company of the delectable Max.'

'Ah, but you've overlooked the fact that the also delectable Amanda will be there,' retorted Abby, grinning. 'Though I suppose it's worth going just to see how she behaves towards our resident cartoonist when her husband's around.'

'Like that, is it?' chuckled Julie, rolling her eyes.

Worried in case she had been indiscreet, Abby shook her head. 'No—it was just me being catty. But you know what a flirt Max is—and she's just as bad.'

'The irritating thing about his flirting is that he does it so painstakingly selectively,' laughed Julie, making her way to the door. 'I take it you've noticed that he only indulges in it when he knows he's absolutely safe—which is probably why he hasn't flickered so much as an eyelid in my direction; he knows darned well I'd be all over him like a rash given the slightest encouragement. Anyway—thanks for the coffee; and enjoy yourself tonight, for heaven's sake!'

'I'm sorry it was such late notice,' a somewhat tired-looking Max apologised when he picked her up that evening. 'Jack Morrison contacted me last week about it, but it simply slipped my mind.'

'Not to worry,' said Abby, the stiltedness of her words bringing it home to her how acutely ill at ease she was feeling. Not that she had ever felt in the least at ease in his presence, she reminded herself gloomily.

His eyes flickered impersonally over her as he helped her into his car, but it wasn't until they were on their way that he spoke.

'Your hair's different.'

'I often wear it like this in the evenings,' she lied, riled by the non-committal indifference of his tone and annoyed with herself for actually having gone to the trouble of weaving a couple of experimental plaits into her hair. 'Where exactly are we going?'

'To Gladstones—we're meeting them there,' he replied, then added with a grim lack of humour, 'I hear it's the place to be seen in at the moment.'

Abby's heart sank; she had never heard of the place but was already beginning to wonder if she shouldn't have chosen something a little more dressy than the deceptively simple Italian silk jersey dress she had, after much uncharacteristic dithering, decided on. Irritated to discover how rapidly her already depleted confidence was waning in the face of the particularly uncommunicative mood he was in, she reminded herself how good she normally felt in the figure-skimming sage-green dress—and also of the small fortune it had cost her the previous year.

'I'd be grateful if this evening didn't become too protracted,' he muttered, after a silence so lengthy it was verging on hostile. 'I've a plane to catch tomorrow.'

'That's fine by me,' replied Abby tartly, 'because I have a job to get to in the morning—I prefer doing my socialising during the weekends.' Which wasn't really true, she admitted reluctantly to herself, but she wasn't looking forward to this evening in the least—especially with him in this mood—so why pretend she was?

'It's the only night I had free this week and Sir Jack's off again next week, so there wasn't much choice,' he replied indifferently. 'But do feel free to class it as business, if it makes you feel better about it—all they wanted was to show their appreciation over the Richmond place.'

'If that's the case,' retorted Abby, knowing full well it must be, 'I'm hardly the one they should be wining and dining. Peter did all the design work.'

'Poor Peter,' he drawled. 'I'm sure he'll never forgive us for reaping the rewards of his talent. Good—a parking spot practically on the doorstep,' he added, swinging the car into it.

The Morrisons were at the restaurant bar and it was Amanda who spotted Max and Abby as they were being relieved of their coats, leaping from her stool with cries of delight and rushing towards Max, whom she grabbed by the hand and dragged towards her waiting husband.

Abby finished handing over her coat and found herself offering up a silent prayer as she followed them—if Sir Jack Morrison turned out to be a possessive man they could well be in for a calamitous evening.

Much to her amazement, Sir Jack was smiling as they reached his side and he was the sort of man, Abby quickly realised, whose Press photographs did him no justice at all. He was tall, perhaps a fraction under six feet. He was also a slim, very attractive man who, despite a liberal sprinkling of grey in the thick darkness of his hair, looked a good deal younger than his reputed sixty years. But what she was finding most startling about him was his completely unruffled, even somewhat amused reaction to his wife's publicly effusive behaviour towards another man.

'Now, Jack, isn't he every bit as gorgeous as I've been telling you?' exclaimed Amanda, sounding, to Abby's incredulous ears, almost proud as, still grasping Max's hand in hers, she slipped her arm through her husband's.

'Great though my faith is in your judgement in such matters,' murmured Jack Morrison, his grey-blue eyes twinkling, 'I doubt if young Bradley here would take too kindly to my agreeing he was gorgeous. Besides, I'd regard that word far more applicable to the young lady accompanying him.' His eyes still twinkling mischievously, he extended a welcoming hand to Abby. 'I take it you must be Abby...'

'Oh, I am sorry,' exclaimed Amanda contritely. 'I'm forgetting my manners!'

'Never mind, Abby and I are quite capable of introducing ourselves,' he laughed, winking as he bent chivalrously low over Abby's hand. 'Jack Morrison—and just plain Jack suits me fine.'

He was a warm, immensely likeable man, decided Abby with relief as she watched the two men shake hands, an opinion which only strengthened as the evening progressed. But it was an evening during which she found herself mentally reassessing certain conclusions she had drawn and finding the results not in the least complimentary to herself.

What Julie had said only that afternoon, on the subject of Max's flirting, had no more than confirmed what he had tried explaining to her several weeks ago. She had never considered herself to be narrow-minded or prudish, yet she had judged and condemned both Max and Amanda, whose overtly flirtatious behaviour to one another hadn't been affected in the least by Jack Morrison's presence. Not only that, but, no matter what her behaviour towards their handsome guest, it was plain for anyone to see that the only man Amanda Morrison truly had eyes for, and on whose every word she hung, was her easygoing and supremely relaxed husband.

'It's about time I thanked you for all you've done,' Sir Jack said to her, choosing a moment when his wife and Max had become engrossed in Max's doodling on the notepad he invariably carried with him. 'Don't think I don't appreciate what a task you had on your hands.'

'But Peter Simmonds did all the creative work,' said Abby, a little puzzled. 'All I did——'

'All you did was find a way of handling Amanda,' he interrupted with a chuckle.

'But I can't even take credit for that.'

'But at least you'll take credit for discerning how much more at ease Amanda is with men than she is with most women,' he persisted gently, 'and for producing someone like Max to keep her to the agreed plans. Had I known Peter Simmonds wasn't going to be around I'd have rearranged my schedules to make sure I was there to keep her in line.'

'Which, when it comes to it, was what I was there to do,' countered Abby unhappily. 'And you being such a successful businessman, I wouldn't blame you for criticising my lack of professionalism in not being able to get your wife to stick to agreed plans without calling in outside help.'

'Trying to lay down the law, no matter how obvious, to clients isn't a tactic to be recommended in your line of business—and especially not with a client like Amanda, who tends to feel particularly vulnerable when she has to deal with highly successful businesswomen.'

Abby's open look of complete incredulity brought a soft chuckle from the man beside her.

'Abby, I'm telling you that's exactly how Amanda would have regarded you, no matter what impression she might have succeeded in giving you.' He shook his head, his expression one of indulgent amusement. 'I can almost see it—the pair of you facing one another, Amanda quaking in her shoes because she sees a high-powered businesswoman who'll put her down given half a chance, and you because you see a pampered, supremely confident client hell-bent on undermining the authority your youthful inexperience convinces you that you don't somehow warrant.'

'So what on earth are you thanking me for?' croaked Abby, stunned by such perspicacity in a virtual stranger and horrified by her own lack of it over such a lengthy period.

'Abby, I'm thanking you for having the intelligence to accept you needed an intermediary,' he chided gently.

'What are you two whispering about?' demanded Amanda in teasing tones, while Abby gloomily reflected that there was nothing in the entire operation for which she deserved the slightest credit.

'We're sort of discussing Abby's career,' replied Sir Jack, patting Abby's hand. 'I'm sure she'll go far in it.'

'I'm sure she will,' agreed Amanda, flashing Abby a friendly smile. 'Max was telling me you've only been with his sister's company a short while,' she added, 'but that you must be absolutely brilliant as she's never taken on a student straight from college before.'

'You're making Abby blush, my love,' chuckled Sir Jack, taking one of his wife's hands in his, 'but I've no doubt Max is right. Now—who's for more coffee?'

Abby, who had glanced in Max's direction several times since Amanda's disclosure, looked over at him once again.

'Another coffee would be great,' he said, smiling relaxedly at his host, his eyes never once straying in Abby's direction.

Silence hung between them like a heavy shroud as he drove her home later, a silence she was loath to break until she had mentally prepared exactly what she was going to say—to admit.

And it was a silence that kept encroaching on her determined concentration by bringing her the realisation that she couldn't recall a single occasion throughout the evening when he had addressed her directly. He had laughed and joked with the Morrisons, had reminisced with Sir Jack on the horrors of international business trips—but never once had he addressed a spontaneous word to her. Admittedly he had listened attentively whenever an opinion had been elicited from her by their companions and, yes, he had obviously spoken to Amanda in terms of her being talented—but Amanda was given to exaggeration... Subtly, and without in any way alerting their hosts to it, he had virtually ignored her presence.

'Max, I really would like to speak to you,' she told him eventually, then spoiled the effect of those calmly spoken words by blurting out, 'I realise it's probably not convenient for you...I mean, you have a plane to catch.'

'Yes, I have a plane to catch tomorrow,' he agreed, 'but, no, that doesn't make it inconvenient for me to hear what you have to say.' He manoeuvred the car to a halt outside her home. 'Do you intend talking here?' he enquired, switching off the engine, 'or is it to be in more congenial surroundings, over a cup of coffee?'

'Over a coffee,' she replied, weak-kneed with apprehension as she got out of the car.

She was doing the only thing she could do, she remonstrated sharply with herself as her trembling legs only just made it up the drive. She inserted the key in the lock, reminding herself that this was simply a case of one adult, who had seriously misjudged another, doing her duty as a rational human being in admitting that mistake and apologising.

'I like it,' he announced with spontaneous appreciation as he followed her from the hall into the small living-room.

Her eyes flew around the familiar surroundings, pleasure stirring faintly within her as she saw those bright, uncluttered lines through fresh eyes.

'But, I suppose, in a profession such as yours it wouldn't do for you to live in a run-of-the-mill tip,' he added deflatingly.

'Coffee,' she announced with forced brightness, flinging open the gleaming whitewood doors leading through to the kitchen and dining area.

'Coffee,' he agreed mockingly, drawing out one of the dining chairs and sitting himself down on it, his coolly watchful eyes following her into the open-plan kitchen and remaining on her as she made a pot of coffee.

'Tell me, Abby,' he enquired after a while, 'do you really have something to say to me, or have you lured me into your delightful lair simply to have your wicked way with me?'

She picked up the tray and took it into the dining-room.

'There are things I feel it my duty to say to you,' she told him quietly, placing the tray on the table, 'though remarks like the one you've just made don't make saying them any easier.'

'What makes you think I'd want to make anything easier for you?' he asked contentiously.

'For heaven's sake, Max, are you going to hear me out or not?' she exclaimed, trying desperately to hang on to her control.

'To be perfectly honest, I'm not in the least sure I want to hear your confession,' he muttered, leaning over and helping himself to coffee. 'And it is, I take it, a confession you're about to subject me to,' he added harshly.

Momentarily at a complete loss for words, Abby too helped herself to coffee, then sat down with it at the opposite end of the table to him.

'Max, whatever your reasons, you helped me out at a time when I really needed it,' she began carefully. 'I'm more grateful than you can imagine for that, but I...I've been under a certain amount of...' She broke off with an exclamation of frustration; the last thing she intended doing was trying to make excuses for herself. 'Look, all I'm trying to say is that I owe you an apology!'

'Me?' he exclaimed, looking a little startled. 'If you've anything to apologise for, are you really sure I'm the one you should be addressing?'

'I can hardly start apologising to Amanda, can I?' she snapped irritably. 'Fortunately I had the sense not to let her see the extent to which I was misinterpreting your behaviour towards one another!'

He drained his cup and replaced it on the tray, the look on his face one of complete mystification when he eventually spoke. 'Abby, what the hell are you drivelling on about?'

'About how mean-minded and small I felt tonight when I saw Jack Morrison's complete lack of reaction to you and Amanda behaving as you always have done.'

'You mean, don't you, that, contrary to your expectations, he neither frothed at the mouth nor had an apoplectic fit at the sight of his wife indulging in patently harmless flirtation with another man?' he enquired grimly.

'No, I... I suppose I expected you both to act differently with him around,' she admitted miserably.

'Because you were convinced we had something to hide,' he pointed out coldly. 'Paradoxical though it may sound, there can be such a thing as relatively non-sexual flirting between the sexes—something I've already attempted to explain to you, but with little success.' He gave an exasperated shake of his head. 'For heaven's sake, Abby, I'm not denying that there are some people so possessive that they can't handle those they care about being involved in anything even as harmless as that.'

'Max——'

'I haven't finished,' he countered frigidly. 'And obviously, had there been the remotest chance of Jack Morrison being that type I would have behaved more circumspectly.' He gave another exasperated shake of his head. 'Tell me, Abby, would it offend your sensibilities if I were to describe some of the interchanges between you and Jack this evening as mildly flirtatious?'

'For heaven's sake, can't you understand I'm trying to tell you you're right?' she burst out agitatedly. 'I'm trying to apologise! I'll just have to agree to differ with you over your definition of flirtation, but I realise your behaviour with Amanda was perfectly above-board and I was completely wrong in my interpretation of it.' She broke off, forced to take a gulped breath. 'I'm not normally as insensitive as I must have seemed... I completely misread Amanda.'

'Would you have believed me if I'd tried telling you that she was acting the way she was because she felt intimidated by women like you?' he asked, helping himself to more coffee.

'I'd have found it very difficult,' admitted Abby miserably.

'You should have tried putting yourself in her place,' he said, 'an averagely successful model who falls in love with a well known, wealthy widower quite a few years her senior. Hell, Abby, even you must have some idea what sort of treatment that marriage was subjected to by the gutter Press,' he exclaimed angrily. 'It would take a pretty tough cookie to come through that with her self-confidence intact.'

'And Amanda isn't really all that tough,' sighed Abby, experiencing an unexpected pang of protectiveness towards the woman she could once have cheerfully strangled.

'No,' he agreed, 'but one way or another she's managed to ride above all that was dished out to her, mainly because of the strength of her love for Jack and also, I suspect, because she's one hundred per cent certain time will prove those muck-rakers wrong.'

'It was Jack who explained to me that she feels intimidated by women she regards as high-powered professionals... He immediately knew that that was the last way I would expect anyone to regard me.' She broke off, hesitating before continuing. 'He saw that in me, and you saw Amanda as she really is... and probably knew how much she loved her husband even before you'd seen them together. But how did either of you see all that?'

'Abby, you really do have an awful lot to learn about people,' he sighed. 'Even if Amanda's every other word hadn't been her husband's name, it was still blindingly obvious—though admittedly perhaps not to you—that she loved him.'

'Why not to me?'

He gave her an amused, slightly quizzical look. 'Whether you intended her to be or not, Amanda was perfectly aware you thought we were up to no good, which was why she tended to ham it up somewhat whenever you were in earshot.'

'I'm not sure I wouldn't have done the same thing in her place,' she admitted a trifle ruefully. 'But you're right, Max, I probably do have a lot to learn about people, but I feel I've gone a little way to doing so this evening...and that's why I'd like to apologise most sincerely.'

His reaction was to give her a long, disconcertingly inscrutable look, which he held for several seconds before speaking.

'Abby, it would be most unwise of you to start regarding me as whiter than white simply because you misjudged me over my intentions towards Amanda,' he warned abruptly. 'My intentions towards you haven't altered and they, remember, are of an entirely different nature.'

'Thanks for reminding me,' retorted Abby, her cheeks crimson as she leapt to her feet and picked up the tray. 'Silly me...I actually thought you'd come to your senses and accepted that people simply can't be made to fall in love to order—especially not against their will!' Flashing him her most withering look as he too rose to his feet, she turned and marched into the kitchen.

'I can't think what gave you that impression,' he remarked from unnervingly close behind her as she placed the tray on the worktop beside the sink. 'Or perhaps it's because I haven't been paying you as much attention as you'd like me to?' he taunted softly, his arms sliding around her from behind and sending wave after wave of trembling awareness washing through her as they pinioned her against the solid warmth of his body.

'Why are you doing this to me?' she protested raggedly, hating her own body for the urgent need now pounding inexorably through it.

'Abby, you really must learn not to look at life from such an exclusively personal angle,' he reprimanded in tones verging on being pious. 'You have to realise that whatever I do to you I'm also doing to myself,' he added, his words now a caressing softness against her temple, his hands instruments of sweet torture as they splayed open to slide slowly down her body. 'And I can't say I resent this mutual effect we have on one another any less than you do.'

'All you have to do is keep away from me,' she protested in a voice distorted beyond recognition, 'then we'd both be happy!'

'Stop being so damned simplistic,' he protested with a hoarse chuckle. 'And do you honestly think I haven't tried keeping away from you?' He turned her in his arms, his eyes glowering down at her when she at last faced him. 'I hope for both our sakes it isn't so, but I've a nasty feeling you could be wrong about people not falling in love against their will.'

'I don't care what you think—I'm not going to fall in love with you!'

There was a brooding darkness in his eyes as he listened to the words that had begun in her as a fierce protest and ended in an uncertain croak.

'There you go again—looking at things from an exclusively personal angle,' he sighed, an oddly tentative gentleness in his fingers as they reached up and touched one of the plaited strands in her hair. 'But then I've been known to be disgustingly egocentric at times—which is probably why the question of your falling in love with me, or not, is the least of my worries right now.'

The soft laughter that followed his words so distracted her that he was kissing her before it had registered with her that he was about to do so.

'Put your arms around me, Abby,' he coaxed huskily against her off-guardedly compliant lips, 'and tell me that I wouldn't be making the biggest mistake of my life if I were to fall in love with you.'

Putting her arms round him was something she had begun doing even as he asked, but answering his bemusing question was rendered an impossibility by the single-minded urgency with which they were suddenly touching, tasting, exploring, their actions like those of ones possessed.

She wanted to become part of him, to feel the vibrant warmth of his body beneath her hands, yet she sensed his resistance in the deliberate hunching of his shoulders as she tried to slide her hands beneath his overcoat. Almost fighting him, she tried again, spurred by the inciting heat of the mouth that plundered in rampant hunger against her own.

'No—I have to go!' he groaned, his hands reaching up and trapping hers to stillness, though his mouth instantly resumed its ardent exploration of hers.

'Your plane,' she choked, the words forming themselves independently of her befuddled mind. 'You mustn't be late.'

'What?' he muttered dazedly, his mouth roaming from her lips to explore in restless, random kisses against her face.

'Your plane,' she gasped, tugging frantically to free her hands so that they could hold him as she wished. 'The one you're catching in the morning.'

'But I'm not catching it in the morning,' he exclaimed, lifting his head and drawing down her imprisoned hands to form a barrier between them.

'But you said you were,' she protested, her problem less with his apparent lie than with the unwelcome interruption being brought about by this irritating discussion.

'I said I was catching a plane tomorrow,' he said, laughter creeping into the breathless distortion of his words.

'But you implied . . .' She broke off, part of the mind-numbing madness dying in her as the outlandishness of such an exchange began registering with her.

'Did I?' he asked, laughter still evident in his voice. 'Perhaps I was subconsciously hedging my bets.'

'So that you'd have a built-in excuse to leave?' demanded Abby accusingly, ignoring that part of her begging her to have no more to do with this ludicrous conversation.

'You should know me better than that, Abby,' he chuckled with lazy unconcern. 'If I want to go—I go.'

'Well, go, then!' she flared, renewing her attempts to free her imprisoned hands. 'And stop laughing!'

'What do you expect me to do—cry?' he demanded indignantly, stepping back from her as he suddenly released her.

'You're not right in the head,' she groaned disbelievingly, leaning back heavily against the sink top. 'And I'm beginning to suspect I'm not either,' she added, then astounded herself by bursting out laughing.

'Oh, Abby,' he chuckled, taking a step towards her. 'You... oh, hell!' He pulled himself up abruptly, ramming his hands deep into the pockets of his overcoat as the laughter died on his face. He turned and began walking towards the doors. 'Let's just hope you never give me any reason to make you cry,' he called over his shoulder, then disappeared through the doors.

CHAPTER FIVE

PETER SIMMONDS pursed his lips as he glanced at his watch. 'We've a slight problem, love, in that I'm due for one or two calls concerning the Freeman job shortly,' he said.

Jennifer Bradley flashed him an apologetic look.

'Sorry, Peter, I didn't mean to ramble on quite as I have,' she said, consulting her own watch. 'We've still so much to get through,' she added anxiously.

'How about if I deal with the Freeman calls?' offered Abby. 'Peter can fill me in on the rest of the meeting.'

Jennifer flashed her a look of relief.

'Abby, you're a treasure,' she exclaimed, then turned to Peter. 'Would that be OK with you?'

'It's fine by me, and Abby's got the Freeman files anyway,' he said, then turned to Abby with a teasing grin. 'So off you go... treasure, and I'll fill you in later.'

'And I'll pop in to see you once we're through here,' Jennifer called after her as she left.

It was such a relief to have Jennifer back to her old friendly self, thought Abby as she returned to her office.

'Sally, you can put any calls for Peter through to me here,' she told the switchboard operator.

'Thank heavens for that,' groaned the girl. 'I've practically a full message pad here for him and the others. How long is that meeting likely to go on?'

'Some time yet, I'm afraid, but if there's anything you feel you can't deal with put it through to me and I'll have a bash,' Abby offered, then laughed as she once again found herself being described as a treasure.

She leaned back on her chair and only then admitted to herself how nervous she had been at the prospect of meeting Jennifer again. But the Jennifer who had bounced in this morning had radiated good health and contentment, a fact that made Abby realise exactly how much below par the older woman must have been in those strained weeks prior to her taking time off.

At least she felt good about one Bradley, she thought, her face suddenly clouding. But it was the ringing of the telephone beside her that halted any further examination of that contentious thought and which kept it at bay for the best part of an hour with its more or less constant demands on her attention.

She was just taking advantage of the first real lull she had had in the calls by returning several files to their cabinet when she heard a tap on her door.

'Come in,' she called, slamming shut the drawer, then glanced up to find the tall figure of Paul Lawson in the doorway.

'I thought I might as well have one last stab at making my peace with you,' he announced quietly. 'Though I don't intend making an issue of it—so, if you'd rather not speak to me...'

'Paul, I most definitely want to speak to you,' exclaimed Abby, with a fervour that plainly surprised her visitor. 'I...I can't believe how badly I behaved those other times,' she stammered, guilt rampaging through her. 'I...look, I was just about to have a coffee; will you join me?'

He nodded and, still looking somewhat surprised, took a seat as Abby went to the percolator.

'I came to fetch Jennifer—though I suppose the meeting could go on for some time yet.'

'She's determined to tie up all the loose ends before you whisk her off to the Caribbean. Heavens, how I envy you both!'

'It's a while since we've had a holiday where we can just laze around doing nothing and being together,' stated Paul almost formally, plainly still a little thrown by his genial reception.

'And now's the time to take it, when she's over the morning sickness and hasn't yet begun waddling—to quote your obviously delighted wife.' Abby smiled, handing him a mug of coffee. 'Paul, my warmest congratulations—I'm so happy for you both.'

'You'll forgive me if I admit to being a little puzzled,' he replied a touch wryly.

'I'm hoping you'll be the one forgiving me,' sighed Abby, taking a seat. 'There's so much I want to say to you, but I'm not too sure where to begin.'

But she found a place, darting backwards and forwards from it, often disjointedly, till she eventually arrived at the last conversation she had had with Elaine.

'I just wish I'd had the sense to see things as they so plainly were then,' she whispered miserably. 'Even when you and she became engaged...instead of feeling vaguely disappointed to learn that you hadn't actually popped the question, let alone got down on your knees, I should have been wondering how two people could sort of slip into being engaged, as Elaine seemed to be saying...'

'Abby, had you been a little older, or perhaps had I known you better, I'd have tried talking to you about Elaine's problems—and long before I ever met and fell in love with Jennifer.'

'Elaine admitted that what she needed at the time was professional counselling.'

'And perhaps, had I not let her use me as a crutch for so long, she would have sought it,' said Paul quietly.

'For heaven's sake, Paul, you're the last person who should feel any guilt!' exclaimed Abby. 'You stood by her because you felt she needed you. Most men, trapped as you were, would have run a mile!'

'At the time I realised that my falling in love with Jennifer had only brought things to a head a little sooner than would have happened, though her refusing even to talk things over with me, once I'd told her, worried me desperately.' He gave her an almost shy smile. 'I can't tell you how pleased I am that things have turned out so well for her. I heard she went to Canada and I'd always assumed you'd gone with her... I'm afraid I over-reacted when I discovered you here and you refused to speak to me. For a while I had myself convinced that...well, that things hadn't turned out too well for her.'

'Oh, Paul, I'm so dreadfully sorry,' whispered Abby. 'Max told me that you and he had been worried about Jennifer—the last thing you needed was me turning up, all bitter and twisted, and complicating matters.'

'You weren't to know, Abby,' he replied with a rueful shrug. 'Jennifer and I are all too aware how lucky we are in having found one another...but for a while I found myself wondering about Elaine and asking myself if I actually deserved all the happiness we have.' He gave a smiling shake of his head as Abby began a horrified protest. 'I promise you it didn't last long. I think that, deep down, my real worries were concerning Jennifer, but I wasn't able to face them. She had a nasty bug several months before she became pregnant which left her rather run down. As she'd never really picked up fully, I suppose it was only natural that we were both a little apprehensive when we heard the wonderful news about the baby—not that either would admit it to the other.'

'Well, one thing's for certain—Jennifer is positively blooming with good health right now,' said Abby, then groaned as the telephone rang.

Paul rose to his feet as she dealt with the call, miming to her that he would have to go.

'Why don't you wait for Jennifer here?' she suggested, once she had finished. 'She promised to pop in after the meeting.'

Paul consulted his watch, then shook his head apologetically.

'I've a feeling we're going to end up running a bit late,' he told her. 'I think I'll take myself off to her office and wait for her there—I've a few calls I still have to make. Mike, my brother, is one of my partners now and I'm leaving him in charge of the practice while I'm away.' He rolled his eyes in mock fear.

'You always said he'd make a good lawyer,' Abby reminded him with a smile, 'so I'm sure your practice will be in good hands.'

'I'm certain it will,' he laughed, 'but I keep remembering things I've forgotten to tell him.' He tilted his head to one side as Abby walked round the desk to join him, then gazed down at her with affection. 'You know, Abby, I'm glad we were able to have this chat,' he said, slipping his arm around her shoulders. 'And you be sure to give Elaine my very best wishes for her future happiness,' he added, suddenly sweeping her up in a bear-like hug.

'I most certainly shall,' promised Abby, a lump coming to her throat.

'I must be keeping you from your work,' apologised Paul, releasing her and turning towards the door that had suddenly been flung open behind them but which was now being drawn briskly shut. 'Would you like me to catch whoever that was?'

Abby shook her head. 'They'll probably pop back again later,' she smiled. 'Anyway, off you go and make your calls, then you can put your law practice out of your head and concentrate on having a wonderful holiday and taking good care of Jennifer.'

'I fully intend doing just that,' he chuckled, walking towards the door and opening it. 'And remind that wife of mine, when she turns up, that she has a husband languishing in her office, will you?'

'So—what do you think?' asked Peter Simmonds, grinning broadly at Abby across his paper-strewn desk.

'Peter, I...I can hardly believe it,' breathed Abby rapturously. 'I have to admit that Jennifer did drop a few hints last week before she left...but this?' she croaked. 'It's the sort of job I'd expect the rest of you to be fighting over, not giving to me!'

'Don't get carried away, love. Virtually unlimited funds certainly make any job attractive, but it's not exactly Buckingham Palace you're dealing with and being stuck down in the wilds of Cornwall at this time of year isn't most people's cup of tea,' laughed Peter. 'Though Malcolm was very keen, I must say—in fact he's been down there—but that Scottish project of his is too big a job, and also too far away, for him to attempt tackling both.'

'Heavens,' gulped Abby, her enthusiasm refusing to be dampened. 'Me being given a job that Malcolm Rogers had his eye on!'

'OK, it's the job of the decade,' teased Peter affectionately. 'So remember that even if Uncle Peter won't be looking over your shoulder as he has till now his hand's always available for you to grab should ever you feel the need—not that any of us thinks you'll need it,' he laughed, then added seriously, 'Abby, you're a fully fledged member of the team now and, believe me, we know you can produce the goods, otherwise we'd never have employed you in the first place.'

Needing time to recover from the effect those words were having on her, Abby picked up one of the photographs of the stone-clad cottage that was to be her first major assignment and examined it minutely.

'It really is beautiful,' she sighed. All right, so it wasn't exactly the assignment of the decade, but it was all hers. 'It's a shame we haven't any shots of the interior.'

'I don't think Malcolm took any, but you could ask him,' said Peter. 'He and one of the structural engineers spent a couple of nights there last week and confirmed that it can't be faulted structurally. With that side of it sorted out, it means you'll be going down there on your own—will that be all right with you?'

He laughed as Abby rolled her eyes in protest at the very idea of his asking such a question.

'Did Malcolm and the engineer stay on the actual premises?' she asked.

Peter nodded. 'The last occupants left a few furniture basics there and Malcolm's had the electricity reconnected. The nearest hotel's about ten miles from the property, but that can't be helped. We'll get you booked in...'

'You'll do no such thing,' protested Abby indignantly, not in the least deterred by the idea of a spot of rustic living. 'There's no point my being stuck in a hotel miles from the property when I could actually stay there. I can easily take bed linen——'

'Abby, there's——'

'Peter, you're only saying that because I'm a woman,' she exclaimed. 'And I'm sure if Jennifer or Moira Cunningham were doing this job they'd rough it at the cottage. I'll have a portable telephone with me and it shouldn't take me too long to draft my plans and then I'll have the workmen with me most of the time.'

'I'm glad you mentioned the work-force,' muttered Peter, rummaging through a tray on his desk and producing a file. 'I wanted to run through the major trades with you, just to give you an idea what's on hand,' he said, joining her at the other side of his desk and opening up the bulky file.

It was Bradley Designs's policy, wherever possible, to use local tradesmen. It was files such as this one, meticulously and comprehensively compiled, detailing tried and tested trades and craftsmen of the calibre required by Bradley's, that was one of the factors enabling the company to maintain its uncompromisingly high standards throughout the length and breadth of the country.

'It looks as though just about all that could be needed will be virtually on hand,' enthused Abby, then added excitedly, 'I can't wait to get moved in and started!'

'I still think the hotel——'

'Peter, stop being so prehistoric!'

'OK, have it your own way,' grumbled Peter. 'But promise me that if camping on the premises doesn't live up to your plainly masochistic expectations you'll move into the hotel.'

'I promise,' vowed Abby, then quickly changed the subject before he changed his mind. 'By the way, you never did mention the name of this wonderful client who's prepared to let me have such gloriously free rein with his property.'

'I believe it's someone closely connected with the Bradley family—though Jennifer didn't actually say who,' replied Peter vaguely. 'And as for having free rein, you actually will have a lot more than you would with the average job, but keep it in mind that it will be Max who has the final say now that Jennifer won't be around.'

'Max?' croaked Abby, her entire system giving a convulsive hiccup at the sound of the name she had almost succeeded in convincing herself had been relegated to where it belonged—out of her mind.

'Come on, Abby,' chuckled Peter. 'You know Max—he's hardly likely to interfere. He'd be the first to admit he has little or no interest in this sort of thing. Mind you, he has impeccable taste, but then so have you—so the last thing I envisage is any problem.'

Of course he was right, Abby remonstrated with herself, and there would be little opportunity for Max to interfere even if he wanted to—not with him in London and her in the depths of Cornwall.

'Talking about Max reminds me,' Peter was continuing. 'Now that he's back at his studio, I'll be moving into Jennifer's office and you'll be having this one. Quite frankly, I can't stand all this moving around, but when Julie cracks the whip we all jump—I believe she has plans for your office, though I've no idea what.'

Abby composed her face into a suitable expression, while inside she struggled to regain the feelings of elation that had so suddenly deserted her.

The cottage lay along five winding miles of what only an unusually vivid imagination would term a road. Surrounded by trees and open farmland, it stood in about half an acre of unkempt land, bordered on three sides by piled stone walls. If there had been a fourth wall at the back of the property, it had long since tumbled off the edge of the bank sloping gently to the shingled beach below.

Though she had been feeling pretty tired after her long drive, Abby had felt her spirits start to revive at her first glimpse of the place, then positively lift as she stepped through the front door and into a large rectangular hallway.

The main living areas led off from doors to the left and right of her, separated by a large kitchen overlooking the back of the house and the sea. There were two sets of narrow stairs leading to the upper floor, one on either side of the kitchen door facing her as she entered, an indication that two cottages had been knocked into one, though probably no later than the turn of the century.

Upstairs she found almost the same pattern as that of the rooms below, three surprisingly large bedrooms above the kitchen and living-rooms and a good-sized, though primitively appointed bathroom above the hallway, with a narrow corridor linking the two staircases.

She was grinning delightedly to herself as she took her luggage into the back bedroom—the one that contained the only two available beds—imagining the fun children would have charging up one flight of stairs, along the dark, narrow corridor and down the second flight.

That first day, she simply wandered from room to room, soaking up the feel of the place and, when night drew in and she closed the shutters of the curtainless windows, deciding that her first priority the next morning must be to see about getting a fire going—with the wind howling and the rain lashing against the windows, she had begun feeling decidedly chilly.

It was the cold that drove her to bed far earlier than she would normally have gone, but, snuggled under the duvet she had brought down with her, she began sketching out tentative plans in her head. It was only then that she began wishing she knew the person for whom she was working. Though it was the house itself that would be her principal guide, there were areas of detail where knowing the age and sex of the client would have been useful. Though had it been that important, she immediately reassured herself, Jennifer would certainly have provided such information.

It was then that a picture of Max blasted its way into her mind, its brooding, disruptive image shattering her mood of cosy speculation. Brief though his presence had been in her life, its effect on her, for reasons she was still unable to fathom, had been little short of cataclysmic. She needed time—however much time it would take—to regain her equilibrium, she told herself with a shiver of disquiet, and, perfectionist though she was where her work was concerned, even the idea of consulting Max about her client filled her with dread. In fact, she felt certain she wouldn't be able to bring herself to do so, she admitted with an audible groan—which was not only grossly unprofessional, but also downright ridiculous!

Uttering another, even louder groan, she flung herself angrily on to her other side. He had managed to get under her skin in a way she would never have dreamed possible—and with such humiliating ease! All right, so she had seriously misjudged certain aspects of his character, she conceded as a sensation of bruised vulnerability engulfed her completely, and not least in that there had been times when she had almost begun to believe that he was as caught up as she had been by the ferocious intensity of the attraction between them. But the truth was that she had been incredibly naïve, she accepted, curling up into a tight ball of seething mortification beneath the duvet. Max was an experienced man of the world who amused himself by collecting the female scalps so plainly there for his taking... and it was a pastime he indulged in just so long as it didn't require any real exertion on his part. And that was what had so hurt and humiliated her, she at last admitted to herself—his not having made the slightest effort to contact her once he had returned to his own studio.

No—she wouldn't contact him, even if it meant her doing a less than perfect job here, she vowed as her eyes grew heavy with incipient sleep...because she still wasn't entirely convinced that she hadn't made the fatal error of responding to his shallow sexual game-playing by falling in love with him.

CHAPTER SIX

'IF I had been an intruder,' growled Max, unbuttoning his heavy overcoat, 'a fat lot of good it would have done you screaming the place down like that—there's no one within a good five miles of this place to hear you.'

'I wasn't screaming the place down,' shrieked Abby, the terror that had seconds ago reduced her almost to the point of collapse still rampaging through her system. 'And how else could you expect me to react?' she demanded illogically. 'Creeping in here like a... like a... What are you doing here anyway?'

'What the hell do you think I'm doing here?' he retorted uninformatively, his eyes flickering towards the heavy, log-filled wicker basket she had been in the process of dragging into the room before abandoning it in the terror of discovering she wasn't alone. 'And what the hell do you think you're doing lugging a weight like that around?' he demanded. 'You could have damaged your back and then what would you have done—crawled five or six miles for help?'

'I asked you what you were doing here,' repeated Abby, her voice high-pitched with the remnants of shock.

His initial reply was to flash her a scowling look as he removed his coat and slung it on to one of two monolithic armchairs, the only items of furniture in the room apart from a badly chipped ceramic-topped coffee-table.

'That's the question I'm here to ask you,' he eventually flung back at her. 'Just what the hell do you think you're playing at, Abby? It's still early afternoon and already it's pitch-dark—and, what's more, it's freezing. Damn it, why can't you behave like any normal person and stay at the hotel?'

'You mean why can't I behave like any normal *woman*, don't you?' exploded Abby. 'It's amazing how nobody objected to Malcolm and——'

'Malcolm!' roared Max. 'Until Julie put me right, I was under the impression this was his job!'

'For heaven's sake, it wasn't any secret I've been given it,' exclaimed Abby. 'If you'd spoken to Peter——'

'I haven't had a chance to speak to him; we've both been away. Does he know you're camping here?'

'I'm not camping, I'm——'

'Damn it, Abby, does he know?'

'Of course he knows. He——'

'Well, he must be as big a fool as you are!'

'Max, you might be the person who has the last say about this job,' she informed him frigidly, 'but that most certainly doesn't give you any right to barge in here, shouting and swearing at me.'

'Damn it, I wasn't swearing at you. I...' He broke off with a groan of frustration. 'Abby, no woman in her right mind would stay here; it's...hell, it's primitive and downright freezing!'

'It's only cold because I haven't quite got the hang of lighting the fire yet,' retorted Abby stubbornly, catching hold of one of the basket handles and starting to drag it towards the fireplace. Yesterday she had tried lighting it using only logs from a stock she had found in one of the sheds. Today she had actually been into town and purchased coal and fire-lighters—and still the wretched thing kept fizzling out on her!

'OK—I admit that I'd have no objections to a man staying here on his own,' he bellowed. 'As I've already pointed out, no woman in her right mind would——'

'Have it your own way; I'm not in my right mind!' Abby bellowed back. 'Max, you can rant and rave all you like, but I'm staying here until I've completed my work and nothing is going to alter that fact!'

'Nothing?' he enquired in ominous tones, strolling up to the fireplace and gazing down at her amateurish attempts to re-set the fire with undisguised impatience.

'Nothing.'

'Not even the fact that my chivalrous nature will leave me with no choice but to stay here with you?'

'I'm afraid you'll just have to suppress this so-called chivalry of yours,' retorted Abby, her pulse-rate soaring despite her angry acknowledgement that he was merely indulging in his usual games. 'Unless, that is, you happen to have brought your own bed linen,' she added smugly.

'How remiss of me not to have,' he drawled, then added sharply, 'Abby, what, exactly, are you attempting to do in that fireplace?'

'I'm lighting a fire,' she replied through gritted teeth.

'Well, if that's the way you've been going about it,' he muttered, squatting down beside her, 'no wonder the thing keeps going out on you.'

'If you're such an expert—you do it.'

'Gladly,' he chuckled, elbowing her aside. 'But only on the condition that you move into the hotel.'

'If I intended moving into the hotel, I shouldn't be needing a fire.'

He turned towards her, amusement twinkling deep in his eyes as he chuckled softly to himself and began demolishing her painstaking attempts. As she watched him deftly re-set the fire she fought a silent battle with herself.

She could tell herself all she liked that his intentions towards her were totally dishonourable, that to him sex—a subject he made no bones about being foremost in his mind—was a casual game to be played with any woman who happened to take his passing fancy. She could also tell herself that the only remotely moral aspect of his character was the fact that he didn't dabble in adultery. In fact, she could tell herself such things till the cows came home, she reasoned disconsolately, but it wouldn't lessen one iota the exhilaration, the crazy, stomach-churning, heart-stopping excitement that his company now, and always had, generated in her.

She was deranged, she decided, completely and utterly deranged. It was with that hardly comforting thought in her mind that she turned slightly, catching sight of the perfectly chiselled profile of the man beside her and watching as he put a match to the fire and then sat back on his haunches while he waited for it to take.

Even in her teenage years it had always taken more than mere good looks in a man to attract her, she protested in silent desperation as a hot, aching need throbbed to inexorable life within her—yet what exactly was there about this man, apart from his devastating looks? All right, so she admired the savage humour of his professional work, as did countless others, but since actually meeting him she had been on the receiving end of that lethally barbed humour of his too often to regard it as anything other than warped—so what on earth was there in him to make her feel as she did?

'Now that, my dear Abby, is a fire,' he announced complacently as flames began licking up the chimney and the coals took on a satisfying glow as they settled around the crackling logs.

'It most certainly is,' agreed Abby, the wistfulness that had crept into her words surprising her as much as they plainly did him, judging by the look he gave her.

'My, my, at last we're in agreement,' he drawled, rising to his feet. 'Which is just as well, given that we're to share the same bed linen,' he added, then grimaced with distaste as he examined his coal-blackened hands. 'I hope you've plenty of towels with you—I need a bath!'

Her mind reeling with consternation and fury, Abby leapt to her feet.

'I suggest you have a bath at the same place you'll be sleeping—the hotel,' she informed him in a voice that shook with the superhuman effort she was making to keep her temper under control. 'Though you're welcome to wash your hands before you leave.'

As long as he boiled the electric kettle she had had the presence to bring with her, she thought frustratedly, and silently cursed herself for not having screamed at him to get out—the last thing she wanted was for him to find out about was the ongoing saga of the hot water or, to be more precise, the lack of it.

'Leave?' he murmured, wide-eyed innocence personified. 'My dear Abby, the choice was yours and you made it——'

'Get out of here!'

'Abby, you were the one who pointed out that you wouldn't be needing a fire if you were staying at the hotel...are you now telling me I've gone to all this trouble for nothing—that you've decided to see reason after all?'

'Why can't you get it into your head that I'm staying here and that you're leaving—and leaving right now?' she yelled at him, her temper snapping completely.

'Correction—it's *we* who stay or *we* who leave,' he flung back at her, striding towards her to catch her by the shoulders and pull her roughly against him. 'And you can stop playing so hard to get, darling, because you're just as eager to have me in your bed as I am to climb into it!'

For a split second it was as though her body gave its whole-hearted endorsement to those taunting words. Yet as her every nerve leapt in treacherous welcome to the invasive ministrations of his mouth on hers, it was her pride that belatedly leapt in violent response to the unmitigated arrogance behind both his words and actions. With a strength she had never been aware of possessing, she tore herself free, lashing out with blind rage at his attempts to recapture her.

Anger mixed with surprise in his expression as he reached out, briefly cupping her face in his hands before stepping back from her furiously flailing arms with a shrug of indifference.

'Now we both need a bath,' he taunted carelessly, his eyes flickering in amusement over the dark smudges his hands had left on her face. 'Perhaps you'd care to join me in mine.'

'It would be an insult to an alley cat to compare your morals, or lack of them, to one!' she raged, her starved lungs gulping in air.

'My dear Abby, you really are in a class of your own when it comes to hypocrisy,' he drawled, his eyes suddenly like chips of granite. 'And to think that not so long ago you were patting me on the head and telling me what a good boy I'd been for keeping my hands to myself with Amanda Morrison. Your inordinate preoccupation with the nature of my relationship with Amanda is something that intrigues me deeply... rivets me, you could almost say.'

There was something in those cold, softly spoken words that set Abby's mind searching frantically for their hidden message; knowing him as she did, there had to be one. By the time she felt she had unearthed it, she felt limp and drained and utterly trapped. From the start her every instinct had warned her to beware the powerful attraction she felt towards him. And her every instinct had been right—theirs was the dangerous attraction of complete and utter opposites. Perhaps she was wrong to call him immoral, she argued in her desperation to be scrupulously honest; perhaps it was simply that he was amoral...that morals didn't figure one way or another in his reasoning. Yet he did draw the line at becoming sexually involved with married women, she fretted, though that was a restriction it plainly had never occurred to him to impose on himself where women who weren't married were concerned.

She turned away from his implacable, waiting figure, hot colour replacing the pallor of her cheeks as she realised that she had been no more capable of hiding the inherent jealousy that had been part of her initial suspicions concerning him and Amanda than she had been the magnitude of the attraction she felt towards him.

'My, my, Abby,' he drawled softly, his relentless eyes missing nothing of the agonising consternation gnawing away at her. 'You seem uncharacteristically lost for words.'

And she was, she agreed in silent hopelessness. To him it probably would seem the height of hypocrisy to deny the attraction between them. There were, at a pinch, only two men she could think of with whom she would have welcomed and explored such an attraction...but not with Max. With Max she felt only fear: fear of the brooding, shadowy darkness she had so often sensed in him, but even more so of risking loving a man who, while arrogantly claiming the power to make her want him as she had no other, had baldly declared he would be hers on a temporary basis only.

She held out her hands towards the fire in a reflex response to the sudden aching chill within her.

'It's a waste of time arguing with you, Max,' she stated tonelessly. 'You've obviously made up your mind to stay here no matter what I say. There's a spare bed in the room I'm using. I suggest you bring the mattress down here and keep the fire going—it gets extremely cold at night.'

'Such concern,' he mocked, joining her by the fire. 'Especially towards one who only moments ago called you an unmitigated hypocrite.'

Her shoulders hunched as her body automatically recoiled from his nearness. 'Max, I've already told you—I don't want to argue with you.'

'Why not, Abby?' he demanded harshly. 'Or are you afraid of what might come out in a good, honest-to-God row?'

'I suppose it wouldn't occur to you that it might be you I'm frightened of,' she retorted, her voice trembling with outrage. 'You come barging in here, ordering me around as though I'm some sort of serf. I've made it perfectly plain that I don't want you staying here, but you've made it equally plain that you will—and you actually have the nerve to question my not wanting to argue with you!'

She knew from the palpable tensing of the tall body beside that her words had found their mark, yet there was a part of her that recoiled at such tactics—whatever this danger she sensed herself to be in from Max, it most definitely was not physical.

'For heaven's sake, Abby,' he exclaimed in horror, 'I've a good deal of faults—that I can't deny—but manhandling a woman isn't one of them—no matter how she might incense me.'

Abby gazed down at the fire, furious with herself for the positive twinge of guilt she was experiencing and certain that if she made the mistake of looking at him he would see it in her eyes.

'And God knows,' he continued accusingly, 'you incense me more than any man, woman or child I've ever come across.'

'Of course I do!' she blurted out, then took a gulped breath as she strove to keep calm. 'Max, don't you think it would make life a lot simpler if you and I just accepted that we have nothing whatsoever in common? Half the time you seem to be talking in riddles, for all the sense I can make of what you say... we might just as well come from different planets!'

'What makes you think I want my life simplified?' he sneered.

'You see—there you go again!' she exploded.

'For heaven's sake, where's the riddle in that?' he snapped. 'You should try taking what I say at face value—you might find that works wonders on your powers of comprehension. And as for our having nothing in common—what about what happens between us whenever I take you in my arms?'

'And just how many other women have you that in common with?' she demanded with bitter spontaneity.

'Damn it, don't answer my question with another of your own,' he roared in exasperation.

Her cheeks flushed with resentment, Abby raised her head and flashed him a scowling look.

'You always have to have your own way, don't you, Max?' she accused hotly. 'You wanted an argument and, lo and behold, we're having one!'

He straightened, ramming his hands angrily into the pockets of immaculately tailored trousers.

'If you weren't so hell-bent on avoiding answering the perfectly straightforward question I just put to you, there wouldn't be any argument,' he pointed out coldly, a flash of something comparable to pure loathing cooling the heat of anger in his eyes—a fleeting, disturbing moment that was over even before her heart had finished the sickening plummeting the sight of it had activated.

'I hardly think you need my verbal admission to confirm that I find you physically attractive,' Abby stated tonelessly, shaken to the core by that fleeting moment yet, as she always had on those other occasions, already beginning to question the validity of her interpretation of it. 'And all we're doing is going round in circles . . . we've been through all this before.'

'We've been through *nothing* before,' he contradicted harshly. 'Though not from want of trying on my part. You, needless to say, made snide remarks about my creating an idyllic boy-meets-girl scenario instead of answering the pertinent questions I was trying to put to you through such an—admittedly not terribly apt—example.'

'Your trouble is that you have an exceptionally selective memory,' exclaimed Abby indignantly.

'Is that so?'

'Yes, it is so!' She turned from the fireplace and flung herself down on one of the chairs, all sense of caution deserting her as she finally snapped. 'And, to refresh that oh, so selective memory of yours, your not terribly apt example of the boy-meets-girl routine had, starring in the boy's role, a cynical womanising man whose involvement, you were at pains to point out, would only be passing, and whose idea of a bit of amusement was experimenting to see if he could make the girl fall in love with him!'

'There's nothing wrong with my memory,' he retorted, seating himself on the arm of the second chair and watching her from narrowed eyes. 'Your chronology is out of order.'

'My what? Oh, for heaven's sake!' she yelled, leaping to her feet in complete exasperation. 'Find someone else to play your stupid mind games with—I've had enough of this!'

'That's right, Abby,' he mocked savagely. 'Run rather than face up to anything as distasteful as the facts.'

'Facts?' she almost howled, spinning around in mid-flight. 'The fact is that you don't even *like* me—so what sort of pervert are you that you want to have an affair with me?'

She remained frozen to the spot as he strode towards her and grasped her by the shoulders.

'Abby, why the hell do you think I'm here?' he demanded exasperatedly. 'For heaven's sake, when I first met you I was attracted to you, and, what's more, it didn't exactly require psychic powers on my part to deduce it was a mutual attraction—or do you intend arguing the toss over that?'

She didn't intend arguing the toss over anything; she was experiencing the unpleasant sensations of a pounding head and racing pulses, not to mention an overriding desire to run as fast and as far as her legs would carry her—but she managed a non-committal shrug anyway.

'The one thing that's guaranteed to bring out the worst in me is the knowledge that I'm not being dealt with honestly,' he stated so quietly that Abby unguardedly raised her eyes to his, only to close them instantly against the unexpectedly fierce intensity of his gaze. 'I don't deny saying any of the things you've just accused me of but, if only for the sake of chronological accuracy, I must point out that I said them in the knowledge that you were not being honest with me.'

Her eyes still closed, Abby's mind began reflexly struggling to remember at precisely what point the possibility of loving him had begun panicking her. It was only when it dawned on her that not for a single instant had she experienced the slightest doubt as to the sincerity of his accusation of chronological inaccuracy on her part that she arrived at the only conclusion possible—that the fear must have begun lurking in her subconscious far sooner than she had been aware.

'God only knows what possessed me to think you might start being honest now,' he muttered in disgust, his hands dropping from her shoulders.

Abby's mind was churning in confusion as she watched him stroll back to one of the chairs and fling his long, lean body down on it. Of course he knew how she had reacted to him—he had taunted her often enough with that knowledge, hadn't he?

Her steps uncertain, she walked over to where he sat gazing granite-faced into the glowing fire, desperately trying to bring some semblance of order to the chaos of her thoughts. If, as it seemed to appear, he genuinely wasn't aware of the fears besetting her, what on earth *did* he think? Accepting that something approaching the truth was her only option, she took a steadying breath.

'If you really must know, for a while I was afraid of the possibility of my actually falling in love with you,' she blurted out, then added self-protectively, 'Now, of course, I find the very idea ludicrous.'

She had no idea just what reaction she had expected from him, but his harshly derisive laughter certainly wasn't it.

'Come, now, Abby,' he drawled. 'Surely even you can come up with something a little more convincing than that.'

Dry-mouthed with shock, she instinctively launched into attack.

'I agree that the very idea of any sane woman even temporarily thinking she could fall in love with a creature like you takes some swallowing,' she ground out, 'but we all have our off moments.'

'Ah, but you weren't immediately aware what a loathsome creature I am,' he gibed, 'and besides, you liked me . . . and, I can only assume, still do.'

'You can't assume anything,' she retorted, something in his tone galvanising her to scalp-tingling alertness.

'Now, that really does surprise me,' he said, his tone parodying pious bewilderment, 'considering that you're the one who keeps claiming that only an out-and-out pervert could lust after someone he doesn't actually like—or are you going to tell me I misunderstood what you said?'

Part of her incapable of accepting that this ghastly exchange was actually happening, Abby took a couple of unsteady steps backwards, mercifully encountering the solid arm of the chair as she did so and sinking down on to it weakly.

'Max, why won't you believe me?' she croaked in protest and was both dismayed and angered to hear the note of pleading that had crept into her words—how on earth had she allowed herself to be reduced to pleading with this insensitive oaf?

'Come now, Abby,' he drawled, 'you're not exactly burdened with a crippling inferiority complex where men are concerned, yet you expect me to believe a load of rubbish about the remote chance of your falling in love—with a man, I should stress, who finds you every bit as desirable as you undoubtedly do him—filling you with abject fear!'

'You're twisting my words; I said nothing about——'

'And what the hell are you twisting, Abby?' he demanded harshly. 'Are you saying it's not just me—that the idea of falling in love with *anyone* terrifies you?'

'You're mad—I'm saying no such thing!'

'So what stopped you playing the odds as any normal woman—or man, for that matter—would have?'

'Max, for heaven's sake stop this,' she protested weakly. 'I've no idea what you're talking about.'

'I'm talking about human nature,' he replied contemptuously. 'Apparently it never once occurred to you that if there was a chance of your falling in love with me there might also be a similar one of my falling in love with you...or perhaps I'm simply under a misapprehension as to what actually makes the world go round!'

Abby's eyes were huge with disbelief—he couldn't possibly be that stupid! He was a celebrity, for heaven's sake, a gifted, wealthy, heart-stoppingly attractive man who had women falling all over him yet one who, for all his unspeakable arrogance, had just spoken as though he was oblivious to the fact that a man such as he would seem completely unattainable to someone like her. Her stunned mind see-sawing between rejection and acceptance, she looked over at him. And one glimpse into those glacially contemptuous eyes was all it took to chase any thought of acceptance from her mind.

Perhaps there really were people so supremely self-confident that self-doubt, even in others, was a concept completely beyond their comprehension, she thought numbly. Yet the look of supercilious arrogance with which Max glanced at her before rising to his feet and walking over to stoke up the fire left her with an indelible impression that he was the sort of man who felt others had every right to be riddled with self-doubt in the lordly perfection of his presence.

'Do feel free to change the topic of conversation,' he urged sarcastically, prodding at the fire with one of the smaller logs, 'as I'm beginning to find it boring in the extreme.'

'And you're not the only one,' replied Abby, though how she managed to get the words out she had no idea—she was trembling with fury. 'Perhaps you'd like me to try juggling a few pieces of coal to keep you amused?'

'That won't be necessary,' he murmured, twisting round to sit on the hearth and regarding her with amused detachment. 'What you can do, though, is find me a towel—I'm in even more need of a bath now than I was earlier.'

'There isn't any hot water,' snapped Abby, then added hastily, 'At least, not until I get the range lit.'

'I suggest you go and light it,' he exclaimed exasperatedly, getting to his feet. 'Meanwhile, I'd better get my things in from the car.'

'Exactly how long were you planning on staying here?' demanded Abby angrily.

'I wasn't planning on staying at all until you proved so pig-headed.'

'You just happen to travel around with luggage, do you?' she sneered.

'I "just happen" to have my squash gear in the car, which fortunately includes a couple of tracksuits and other useful items. You'll be glad to hear I shan't need to borrow things like your toothbrush or your underwear.'

The moment she heard the front door close behind him, Abby made her way into the kitchen and approached the huge, oil-fired black range with scowling uncertainty. By the time she had discovered the day before that this was the only means by which the water could be heated, had located the oil tank in the garden then learned from the gauge it was quarter full, half of the day had sped by. The fact that the original ignition instructions on the oil inlet had worn away to illegibility had driven her back to using the kettle until she could seek advice.

'Haven't you got that thing lit yet?'

Abby started at the sound of that hectoring voice from behind her.

'No, I haven't—and, what's more, I haven't the faintest idea how to!'

'That's not the impression you gave earlier,' he murmured, plainly enjoying himself.

'Had I lit the thing straight after coming back from town, I wouldn't have had any problem,' she claimed defensively, not in the least certain it was the truth, what with her unfamiliarity with the local accent and the fact that so many people had joined in with instructions in the hardware shop where she had sought advice that her head had been reeling when she had left. 'There aren't any instructions here,' she snapped in answer to the exaggeratedly bemused look he gave her, 'so I had to ask in town.'

'Oh, I see.' He smirked. 'Your delight at my turning up has driven whatever you learned clean out of your head.'

'That's not quite how I would have phrased it,' she muttered viciously.

'No, I'm sure it isn't,' he chuckled. 'But while you're recovering from whatever it is, you can make yourself useful. There's a fire-guard and a set of fire-irons in the outhouse by the woodshed—you get them while I get this thing lit.'

She was too busy struggling to keep her fury under control, as she located the implements and carried them into the living-room, to give any thought to the preciseness of the instructions she had been given. When she eventually started doing so, she raced back into the kitchen.

'You've been here before!' she accused. 'You knew exactly where those things were!'

'Well, one thing I certainly don't know is how long this thing takes to heat the water,' he muttered, brushing past her and picking up the large black leather sports bag he had deposited in the hall. 'God only knows how long it's likely to be before we're both bathed and ready to eat...I take it the hotel's the only place we'll get a meal around here?'

'Yes, it is,' she muttered vaguely, her entire train of thought disrupted by his disappearing up one of the flights of stairs.

'You'd better ring and book us a table for as late as they'll take us,' his disembodied voice called to her.

'You're most welcome, in the interests of saving both time and water, to join me in my bath.'

Abby flew up the stairs after him and found him in *her* bedroom, his bag on *her* bed and his shirt stripped from him and flung down next to the bag!

'Get out!' she shrieked, uncertain whether to stand her ground or flee as he kicked off his shoes and unzipped his trousers. 'Get out!' she repeated, her rage rendering her immune not only to reason but even to the glorious near-nakedness of the bronzed body revealed as he stepped casually from his trousers.

'Darling, it really isn't the done thing to order a man from his own premises,' he drawled, 'nor, from a purely professional standpoint, to shriek like a fishwife at the owner of the property on which you are working.'

CHAPTER SEVEN

'I JUST rang to hear how you were getting on and also to let you know I'd got my facts wrong about your client—apparently it's Max himself.'

'Tell me something new, Peter,' said Abby into the portable telephone, glowering over at Max's figure sprawled across the armchair a couple of feet from hers, his dark head bent towards the large pad on which he sketched with swift, sure strokes.

'Hello, there, Peter,' he called out on hearing the name, his eyes locked on his work.

'Am I imagining things, or was that Max's voice I just heard?' asked Peter, laughter in his voice.

'Unfortunately, it's not your imagination,' muttered Abby, flashing an angry look in the direction of the man whose presence she didn't find in the least amusing. 'He turned up the day before yesterday.'

'And no doubt ordered you straight into the hotel,' chuckled Peter, then added encouragingly, 'but it must be pretty handy having him around to consult on the odd point or so.'

'I hate to disillusion you, Peter, but Max's only contribution so far has been to mutter "Surprise me" whenever asked for an opinion.' Apart from making concentrating on getting on with her work next to impossible with his disruptive presence, she added silently—though he appeared to be churning out sketches at a remarkable rate, she reminded herself disgruntledly.

'If that's the case, take him at his word, love,' chortled Peter.

'Perhaps I shall,' she murmured, flashing a malicious glance in the direction of her industrious companion. 'And, "surprise" being the operative word, I was thinking along the lines of flock wallpaper and the odd chandelier, but at the moment I'm concentrating on which walls to knock down.'

'Over my dead body,' called out Max, flashing her a grin then returning his attention to his sketch-pad in complete ignorance of the havoc he had just created with her heart-rate.

'Now, now—no bickering, children,' admonished Peter, having obviously heard. 'But seriously, Abby, if Max is happy with what you come up with you'll be able to get cracking at once.'

'What—without you checking it out first?' she blurted out, and immediately felt like kicking herself when she heard Peter's groan of exasperation.

'This is *your* job, love,' he sighed. 'How many times do I have to remind you that you didn't get this job just on the strength of that gorgeous smile of yours?'

'OK, OK, forget I asked,' she begged.

'That's better,' he chuckled. 'Now back to the drawing-board with you, and put Max on to me, will you? I've a nasty suspicion he's fled down there to escape the attentions of the young lady who turned up here looking for him the other day—though why any young man in his right mind would want to avoid a creature of such stunning perfection is completely beyond this middle-aged man's comprehension.'

'I'll hand you over to him,' said Abby, shaken by the sensation of violence knotting within her. 'Give everyone my love—and I'll be in touch soon.'

She handed the telephone over to Max, avoiding any eye contact with him as she did so. Then she picked up a paint chart from the table, holding it like a mask before her as she frantically examined her unpleasant state of mind. It was called jealousy, she informed herself venomously—and all it had taken was one light-hearted reference to Max and another woman for her to become racked with it.

And as for his reason for turning up here, she, despite his every indication to the contrary, had managed to convince herself it was interest in his property. Joking though Peter's suggestion had been, it had a possible ring of truth about it.

'Give this number to her and I'll not be responsible for my actions...no—towards you, you numbskull!' threatened Max into the telephone, laughter in his voice. 'Though if Abby gets to you first, it's curtains for you, old buddy—those green eyes are not to be messed with!'

Abby lowered the paint chart, her green eyes responding with fury.

'I'll be in touch when I'm back in town—we'll have a drink,' he finished off, then handed the telephone back to Abby, amusement twinkling in his eyes as they met and held hers. 'Your jealousy's showing, darling.'

'Fantasise all you like,' retorted Abby coldly, flinging the telephone down on the table, 'but don't you think you've caused enough disruption here without the prospect of one of your put-upon women turning up and adding to it?'

'Suzanna, I can assure you, isn't the least put-upon, and the chances of her turning up here are extremely remote,' he murmured, his expression one of pious innocence. 'Though I'm sure you'll fight like a tigress on my behalf should the unlikely happen.'

Abby opened her mouth to give him a piece of her mind, then clamped it shut. That had been the pattern right from the start, she warned herself bitterly, his tying her up in mental knots, goading her beyond reason, and her inevitably losing her temper... well, not this time!

Conscious that he was lying in wait for her reaction, she once again picked up the paint chart and began studying it intently.

'You know, Abby, there's really no need for you to be so jealous,' he murmured sweetly, tossing his sketch-pad and charcoal to the floor. 'No other woman but you occupies my thoughts right now.'

Because right now she happened to be the only woman around, she added in silent fury, every nerve in her body crying out for retaliation.

'Don't tell me you don't believe that,' he persisted.

'Max, I've work to get on with,' she stated, digging deep into her reserves of control, 'so I suggest that you go into the kitchen and continue this conversation with yourself—because I have no intention whatever of contributing to it.'

'What—you don't want to talk to me?' he exclaimed, contriving to sound mortally wounded.

'I don't want to talk to you.'

'Not even about this place?'

She lowered the chart and glared at him.

'Not even about the kitchen?' he wheedled. 'Abby, yesterday you seemed particularly eager for my opinion regarding the kitchen.'

'I merely enquired whether or not you wanted the range left in it,' she burst out angrily. 'And, as with any other question I've put to you regarding such details, your reply was "Surprise me"!'

'Surprise, darling, not shock,' he sighed, then smiled with a rueful sweetness that didn't fool her in the least. 'All that talk about flock wallpaper and chandeliers frightened the life out of me.'

Abby flashed him her most withering look, then returned her attention to the chart.

'So that's why I've decided to co-operate in any way you wish.'

Abby returned the paint chart to the table, carefully so as not to betray any of the doubts and confusions raging inside her.

'And you honestly expect me to believe that?' she asked tonelessly. 'Max, this might just be no more than another source of amusement to you, but it's my job—something that means everything to me.'

He flashed her an oddly impassive look. 'I've been searching on and off for the best part of a couple of years for a property such as this, so you're mistaken in thinking my attitude towards it is anything other than serious. Time is something I have very little of on my hands—which is one of the reasons I placed it with Jennifer.'

'Yet you've managed to find the time to come down here,' retorted Abby, 'though you might just as well be a passer-by for all the apparent interest you've shown in the place.'

'I don't employ others to do work for me and then expect to end up doing it myself,' he informed her. 'One of the pleasures of my job is that I can do it just about anywhere, something I've been taking advantage of to the full since I've been down here. Don't tell me you hadn't noticed.'

She had noticed all right, she thought bitterly; the ease with which he could become totally immersed in his work, while she sat there tense and distracted and incapable of stringing her thoughts together, had only added to her frustrations. She was just about to ask why he should choose to work in conditions like these, instead of in the comfort of his studio, when something suddenly clicked into place in her mind.

'Why not admit that one of the reasons you came here was because you learned I'd been given this assignment and not Malcolm Rogers, as you'd expected?'

'And what other reasons am I going to be asked to admit to?' he enquired, his eyes sweeping mockingly over her tense figure.

'For heaven's sake!' she exclaimed angrily, refusing to be diverted. 'You've obviously no faith in my ability to do this job, yet when I ask your advice all you come up with is "Surprise me"!'

'Abby, way back in the good old days—when I was still the potential love of your life,' he mocked, 'I seem to remember pointing out to you that you'd never have been employed by Bradley's if you hadn't the necessary skills. OK, so Malcolm did do up my London place and knows exactly what my tastes are, but——'

'But you've no such confidence in me!'

'Either let me finish what I'm saying, or shut up—but don't start putting your words into my mouth,' he snapped. 'You complain when I leave you alone to get on with your job, yet, almost in the same breath, you accuse me of having no confidence in your ability to do so. Abby, it was the character of this place that led me to buy it and, let's face it, it's a character so dominant that even I can see that there's only so much that can be done within its dictates.' He grinned as Abby flashed him a surprised look. 'But that's all I can see, which is why it would be pointless for me to be breathing down your neck and making suggestions while you're drafting your plans. So, when I say I'll co-operate in any way you wish, I mean I'll do so once the plans are finished and I can see the overall picture... Does that make you feel any better?'

Abby nodded, her tentative smile confirming that, oddly enough, the logical reasoning behind his words had made her feel considerably better—from a purely professional standpoint.

'Mind you,' he murmured, his mouth quirking humorously, 'we could well end up coming to blows over the flock wallpaper and the chandeliers.'

'Perhaps not,' she murmured, conscious of how much she was savouring this moment of light-hearted respite. 'Having had second thoughts, I've decided they're not such a good idea.'

'That being the case, I look forward to seeing your plans with nothing but pleasure.'

Abby glanced over at the fire, sorely tempted to prolong this unique interlude of peace while knowing in her heart she had little option but to disrupt it.

'I'll get copies off to you the moment they're finished,' she said and unconsciously began holding her breath as she awaited his response.

'Is that your way of telling me you'll be moving into the hotel?'

'Max, be honest,' she sighed, her body tensing in anticipation of their inevitable return to bickering contention. 'Your coming down here had nothing to do with where I was or wasn't staying. You know you'll be getting the plans as soon as they're drafted, so why not leave me in peace to get on with them in the way that suits me best?'

'*You* are asking *me* to be honest?' He laughed, shifting his sprawled body slightly as he turned to look at her. One of those fleeting expressions she found impossible to fathom flickered across his features as she unflinchingly returned his gaze. 'Whether or not you're prepared to accept that your safety was one of them,' he continued, 'you've already divined that there could be several reasons for my being here.'

'And if there are, my moving into the hotel isn't going to affect them one way or another.'

'Just as it won't affect the fact that I'm a man of my word,' he retorted, only the sudden darkening of his eyes marring the picture of relaxed ease he portrayed.

'So what it boils down to is that you're prepared to sit it out here until you get your own way,' snapped Abby, wondering just how much more she could take of this relentless treadmill of verbal fencing and stress.

'Interpret it any way you wish,' he replied with a shrug.

'Max, you've admitted how long you spent finding this place,' she said—as her pride wouldn't allow her to plead, at least she could try reasoning with him. 'Now that you've got it, surely it's in your own interests to have it habitable as soon as possible.'

'I can see no reason why it shouldn't be habitable according to schedule—not that I'm in any rush to be able to use it. You see, Abby, I'm a city boy and London's where I live, whereas this is to be my bolt-hole—the place to which I can escape when the fancy takes me.' He shifted his body again, this time to throw one long, tracksuited leg over the arm of the chair. 'Am I to take it that you're threatening to go on strike?'

'Your inability to see further than the end of your nose amazes me,' she exclaimed bitterly, the resentment welling up in her directed not only at him but also at the pride in her that made it impossible for her simply to move into the hotel and spare herself any more of this. 'Trust you to think I'm threatening you with going on strike. It simply wouldn't occur to you that you could be the problem—that I simply can't work properly with you around!'

'And I wonder why that could be, Abby,' he murmured, his saccharine tone like salt to a wound.

'You know perfectly well why,' she exploded accusingly. 'I can't think straight with you around—which is exactly the way you want it. Ever since I met you, you've gone out of your way to bait and confuse me. I'm not used to people who enjoy manipulating others just for the hell of it! I'm not used to people who go in for the sort of devious sexual games you seem to thrive on!'

'Devious, Abby?' he murmured. 'There's nothing that could be described as devious in my sexual approach to you—I want you and I've been perfectly honest about it.'

'Stop it!' she cried out. 'You can deny it all you like, but you know perfectly well what I mean! I've told you how much my job means to me...so much that there was even a time when I mistakenly felt I was sacrificing my integrity because of it.'

'How fortunate for you that you were mistaken,' he drawled. 'Or was it simply a question of your integrity losing out?'

'It's easy for you to sneer. You wouldn't know what it's like to be...' She broke off, flashing him a look of pure loathing before leaning her head wearily back against the wing of the chair.

That was the problem when she lost her temper, she remonstrated furiously with herself—her tongue tended to run away with her and she ended up looking a complete fool. He would probably fall about the place laughing at the mere idea of the anguish she had put herself through over her irrational feelings of having betrayed her sister.

'Whatever it was you decided against saying,' he stated eventually, 'you're no doubt right; I wouldn't know what it's like.'

Her head throbbing and her mind reeling, she decided on giving trying to reason with him one more go.

'Max, I want to give of my best in my work here, irrespective of whom the place belongs to... It's just that I honestly don't feel I can in the atmosphere there is between us.'

'So—the only solution is to change the atmosphere,' he stated, rising to his feet and smiling down at her for all the world as though neither had ever raised a voice against the other. 'I'll make us some tea.'

'But you told me you couldn't make tea,' she protested in dazed response to the shock of his actually having made such an offer, then clutched her hand to her head... For the sake of her sanity, she had no option but to pack her bags and go to the hotel!

'No. What I did was imply that I couldn't—a fairly common ploy, I believe, among manipulators who prefer to be waited on,' he explained unabashed, then grinned down at her disarmingly. 'Though I must say I was more than a little disconcerted by the readiness with which you appeared to accept that I actually was that moronic.'

Though unable to conceal her wariness of this sudden switch in his mood, Abby's gaze, as she turned her face up to his, was none the less acutely intent. She discounted the nonchalant stance of his tall, tracksuited figure and the lazy grin adorning his handsome features, seeking out only his eyes. There had been other occasions on which he had appeared much as he did now, but when all it took was one glance into those heavy-lidded, mesmerisingly beautiful eyes to receive a chillingly different message. But this time the contradiction she encountered was of a very different nature from the chilling aggression for which she had instinctively prepared herself—a brooding uncertainty that seemed to reach out and inundate her already beleaguered mind with yet a further barrage of uncertainties.

'I...yes, I'd love some tea,' she stammered, her eyes dulled by perplexity as he nodded and left the room.

She couldn't take much more of this, she told herself weakly... She hadn't the slightest inkling what made this man tick!

Yes, she did, she told herself fiercely, leaping to her feet and throwing all her pent-up frustrations into building up the fire. She knew all she needed to know about him! She was probably only kidding herself imagining there were times when his eyes betrayed him—most of the time he used them in the same calculating way he used every other weapon in his vast arsenal!

Attacking the fire as though holding it wholly responsible for her every woe, she impatiently discarded any thought of attempting to sift through the possible reasons for his presence—the point was that she was stuck with him and, whatever new tactic he came up with, she would be prepared for it.

'Our priority tomorrow has to be to get some decent china and a tray,' he complained, albeit sociably and with a smile blatantly intended to disarm, when he returned with two mugs of tea.

Two could play at this little game, Abby told herself grimly, and smiled equally disarmingly as she accepted the mug he handed her.

'You remind me of my sister,' she confided chattily. 'She can be very pernickety over what she drinks from.' She forced her smile a little wider, worried in case 'pernickety' had sounded a trifle contentious. 'I once gave her wine in a tumbler and she carried on as though I'd asked her to swig it from the bottle.'

'As anyone with a discerning palate would have,' he retorted with a grin, then sat down by the hearth and eyed his own mug with rueful misgiving.

'Well, unlike you and my sister, I'm the sort of pleb who regards tea as tea no matter what she's drinking it from,' she murmured, then took a long, exaggeratedly appreciative drink from her mug. 'Mmm, delicious!'

'There's no need to get quite that carried away,' he said, his smile taking on a rather fixed look. 'Though, if your taste buds are that neglected, perhaps something should be done about putting a bit of culinary education your way,' he continued, obviously having decided that venting his irritability was something he would have to sacrifice in the interests of creating the right atmosphere. 'Which means we'll have to venture a bit further afield than the hotel.'

'What's wrong with the food at the hotel?' asked Abby innocently, perfectly aware that the most charitable thing that could be said about it was that it was patchy in quality.

'What indeed?' he murmured, rolling his eyes. 'Though I have to admit it's a different place altogether when their chef's there—I believe he takes off in the winter.'

'Having a palate as highly developed as yours must create dreadful problems at times, such as these,' sighed Abby, her tone oozing sympathy.

'Is that so?' he queried, amusement lurking in his eyes.

'Oh, yes! I mean, if the worst comes to the worst, I'm quite happy to make do with the local fish and chip shop, whereas someone like you...' She gave an expressive little shrug as she allowed her words to trail away and found that she was almost beginning to enjoy herself—of the two of them, she was willing to bet that his patience would be the first to cave in under this relentless barrage of grating niceness.

'If it's fish you want, there's a very good fish restaurant in Plymouth,' he said, smiling almost as though acknowledging the shamelessness with which he was misinterpreting what she had said. 'We'll try it tomorrow.'

'But, Max, Plymouth's miles from here,' she exclaimed, her lips twitching in response, 'and it's not even in Cornwall!'

'They do say travel broadens the mind,' he murmured, laughter dancing in open challenge in his eyes. 'So, is that decided—we dine in Plymouth tomorrow?'

'Yes... as long as we try the local fish and chip shop the following day,' replied Abby sweetly, while admitting to herself that it might have paid to have taken his pig-headed stubbornness into consideration before entering into a battle like this with him... He would be the first to crack—of that she was certain—but it might take a little longer than she had first thought.

'How could I possibly resist so charming an invitation?' he murmured, rising to his feet. 'But the question that really fascinates me,' he added in tones that instantly triggered off alarm bells in her, 'is how long we'll be able to resist one another's physical charms.'

CHAPTER EIGHT

'WHAT'S up, Abby?' asked Max softly, turning away from the draft plans of the house he had insisted on taping across the living-room door and watching her from sharply enquiring eyes. 'You look troubled, yet I've nothing but praise for your plans and I'm almost speechless with admiration at the way you've drummed up such an impressive work-force.'

'Max, you talk as though I'd conjured them up from nowhere,' protested Abby, moving away from the door as she tried to gather her wits. 'I've been supplied with endless lists of local tradesmen—that's the way Bradley's operates.'

The last thing she had expected was for him to ruffle the fragile peace between them by asking so direct and contentious a question—and, anyway, 'troubled' was far too tame a word for what she was feeling!

'Stop evading the issue,' he insisted, quashing any ill-founded hopes she might have had of his thinking twice about the wisdom of such a question. 'I'd have said everything's going as well as you could possibly have hoped—so why do you seem so gloomy?'

'I'm not, I'm...' She broke off, staring sightlessly down into the glowing coals of the fire and silently cursing herself for having been caught so unawares.

At first she had been constantly on the alert for that moment when his studied geniality would crack...but gradually she had been lulled—most certainly not into any false security, she reminded herself bitterly, because most of the time it had been like living on a knife-edge…

'You're what, Abby?'

'Max, I'm simply trying to concentrate all my thoughts,' she exclaimed, desperately trying to sound reasonable. 'There are so many details to keep in mind…I just want to make sure I don't overlook a single one of them.'

'I'm hardly the sort of man who's going to start frothing at the mouth just because you happen to fall a fraction short of perfection in your work,' he muttered, going over to the small table and starting to sort out some of his own drawings scattered on and around it. 'Hell, even if you'd overlooked something major enough to cause the roof to cave in, I wouldn't carry on as though it were the end of the world.'

'That's not what I meant,' she sighed and found herself torn, as she had so often been on other occasions during the past few days, as to whether he was being as genuine as he appeared, or whether he was actually indulging in his old game of baiting her.

'Don't you think it's about time you started explaining exactly what it is that you mean?' he asked quietly.

Abby froze. This was most definitely a new phase he was shifting them into. At first it had been a game, silently and teasingly acknowledged, and one she had, in her misplaced confidence, almost enjoyed. But it had all changed and from then on her self-confidence had been gradually eroded by the constant vacillating of her mind. Sometimes it was almost too easy to accept him as he appeared: a charming, intellectually stimulating and wickedly amusing companion. Yet there were those other times when an oddly loaded remark, a long, brooding look—levelled at her only on occasions when he was unaware of being observed—or even a slight tensing of his jaw would trigger off that sharp chord of warning in her that kept her hovering on the knife-edge of doubt and confusion.

'I feel I ought to check again with the carpenters and decorators,' she stated woodenly. 'There's a lot of work involved in treating those upstairs floorboards——'

'OK, so you don't intend explaining anything to me,' he interrupted brusquely.

'Max, the last thing I want is them getting under one another's feet,' she replied stubbornly.

'So you have doubts about the competence of Bradley's recommended tradesmen, do you?'

'Of course I don't, I... I'm just being over-cautious, I suppose.'

'I suppose,' he echoed, placing the papers he had gathered up on the chair behind him, then rising and stretching. 'How about if we give your culinary education a rest tonight?' he asked, bestowing on her the most dazzling of smiles. 'I thought we might try the bar food at that pub on the quay.'

'That's fine by me.' Completely nonplussed by that smile, Abby knelt down by the table and began sorting her own papers into a stack.

'Abby, I...'

When he didn't continue she turned and found he was walking towards the door, his drawings in his hand.

'It doesn't matter,' he muttered, turning and catching her bewildered look. 'I'll just go and put these away—then we can go.'

She sat back on her heels once she heard the door close behind him, her expression tense and drawn. He had asked her what was wrong, yet even if she had been certain of what the truth was she could hardly be expected to tell him, she reasoned numbly. She had tried telling him the truth once before...and where had that got her? He had once joked about trying to make her fall in love with him and part of her desperate confusion was the fact that she wasn't entirely certain that he hadn't succeeded. She frowned as she remembered the moment a few days ago when he had casually brushed back the lock of her hair which had fallen forward and obscured his view of the plans they had been perusing... So intensely charged had that instant become that they had both momentarily frozen beneath its impact. It had been he who had broken the spell, she remembered, by suggesting an infinitesimal alteration to one of her plans, but what she remembered most vividly was her own searing disappointment at his having chosen to break that spell. But there had been other such moments in the days that had followed, some of them prolonged almost beyond endurance and during which his eyes had held hers and openly willed her to make the move they both craved.

She rose unsteadily to her feet, racked by the conviction that it was the tenuous yet tenacious core of mistrust that so disturbed and confused her that was her only defence against loving him absolutely.

The wind was scudding past the buildings and out to sea when they left the pub, whipping the mountainous crests of the waves to a foaming white froth in its plundering path.

'I need some fresh air,' announced Max, turning up the collar of his coat as he gazed out over the turbulent sea. 'You can wait in the car, if you'd prefer,' he added, searching in a pocket for his keys. 'I'm going to take a walk down the pier.'

'You're mad,' groaned Abby, drawing the hood of her duffel coat up over her head, 'but I'll join you anyway.'

'If I'm mad, I wonder what that makes you?' he asked as they started off down the pier, but had to repeat himself twice more before she caught his words over the fierce howl of the wind.

At his mimed suggestion, she dogged his footsteps, using the bulk of his body as a wind shield, yet wondering if she wouldn't have been better off alone in the car with her restlessly churning thoughts.

There was a change in him tonight...so marked that for once she wasn't dithering around wondering if it was a figment of her imagination. Except that she was dithering around, she accused herself frustratedly. He wasn't exactly the most predictable man at the best of times, so why should this particular change in his mood be any more disturbing than all the rest? But it was, argued a stubborn inner voice, and yet, like everything else that baffled and troubled her about him, it was nothing that she could even begin to put a finger on.

She drew level with him at the end of the pier, leaning against the railings and watching in fascination as he threw back his head as though revelling in the elements unleashing themselves around them.

No one had any right to affect another human being as he affected her, she thought bemusedly, then harshly reminded herself that it was her own stupid fault for having allowed it to happen in the first place.

'I shall be moving into the hotel in a couple of days—once the work's under way,' she called out to him, forced to yell at the top of her lungs those words that were a taunting reminder of how much she might have spared herself had she swallowed her pride and made that move from the first.

'I was wondering when it would sink in with you that you'd have to,' he yelled back, then added unexpectedly, 'Are you a sea person, Abby?'

Startled though she was by the question, it was one she fully understood, opening up in her the familiar wound she had long since accepted would never fully heal.

'Yes, I am . . . I'm most definitely a sea person.'

'Why so definite?' he asked, turning and leaning back against the rails and looking down at her intently, as though preparing to lip-read her reply if necessary.

'Because it's . . . it was a family joke,' she replied, training her eyes on the inky darkness ahead. 'My mother and sister, who weren't similarly besotted with the sea, used to swear that my father and I showed positive withdrawal symptoms if we were deprived of regular sightings of it.'

She was conscious of his eyes searching her face, but kept her own rigidly trained ahead of her, feeling isolated and vulnerable as she contained her grief.

'So my yen for a place such as the one I found here is something that wouldn't really need much explaining to someone like you,' he eventually said, giving her no chance to comment as he added, 'We'd better head back for the car—the rain's about to tip down.'

Halfway down the pier he turned as the force of the gale hurled her against him, wrapping his arms tightly around her and half carrying, half dragging her the rest of the way to the car.

That moment of acute grief now behind her, it suddenly crossed Abby's mind that any normal couple would be convulsed with laughter as they battled their way to safety, but laughter was something that couldn't have been further removed from the grim set of his features when they eventually climbed windswept and drenched into the sanctuary of his car.

'The next time I claim to be in need of fresh air in the middle of a force-ten gale, I'd be grateful if you'd dissuade me,' he muttered once they were on their way. 'Not that there's any likelihood of there being a next time,' he added bluntly. 'It's high time I got myself back to London.'

Abby had never experienced being kicked in the stomach, but the effect of his words gave her a pretty good idea what it might feel like.

'At least your time here wasn't wasted,' she was amazed to hear herself declare. 'You seem to have managed to do a fair bit of work.'

'An amazing amount of work, in the circumstances,' he drawled, then cursed silently under his breath as they turned down the road leading to the house and the car began skidding in the mud. 'I wonder how often this damned road becomes impassable,' he growled. 'The rain we've had in the past couple of days hasn't been that exceptional, but it's pretty close to being a quagmire already.'

'I'm sure the tradesmen's vans will cope,' murmured Abby, and was once again amazed by her ability to speak so naturally despite the havoc still raging within her.

'Perhaps I should trade this in for a van,' he muttered as they drew up in front of the house, no hint that he intended any humour evident either in his tone or his facial expression. 'I think we should give it a couple of minutes,' he said, scowling in the direction of the river of rain washing over the windscreen, 'just to see if there's any hope of it letting up.'

Abby unbuckled her seatbelt, feeling she would rather drown than endure even a second more of this claustrophobic confinement and fighting an almost overwhelming urge to fling open her door and race to the house.

'At least we've a fire to come home to,' he muttered, turning to face her, 'even if that's just about all we have.'

'Once it's finished it will be beautiful,' said Abby, her body rigid and her eyes gazing as though mesmerised at the sheet of rain streaming down the windscreen.

'Yes... I suppose it will be,' he conceded with little conviction, 'but that's not much comfort right now... Tell me, Abby, are you really as nervous as you look?'

Stung by the open taunting in his tone, she swung round to face him, anger flashing in her eyes. The light above the front door, partially deflected by the bulk of his shoulders, added a chillingly sinister cast to the shadowy darkness of his face.

'I'm not nervous,' she lied, furious with herself for having faced him. 'I... I just don't like storms.'

'Now, that really does surprise me,' he murmured softly. 'Someone who loves the sea being afraid of storms... I love them.'

'Why were you interested in whether or not I was a sea person?' she demanded, using the words as a means of distracting herself from physically lashing out at that coldly taunting face.

'I can't for the life of me think why,' he drawled, then turned and opened his door. 'I think it's about time we accepted that the only thing this rain is likely to do is get worse.'

Abby leapt out and raced to the house. By the time she was inside she was already tearing herself free of her sodden coat, wincing at the wetness that had penetrated the thick material and was fast seeping through to her skin.

Feeling chilled to the marrow, she opened the kitchen door and stepped into the welcoming warmth radiating from the range.

'The intelligent thing would be to finish getting out of your wet things,' came Max's hectoring voice from behind her, 'instead of dripping all over the place in them.'

Abby spun round to face him, her eyes blazing as she watched him carelessly toss his own dripping coat over the door.

'Why don't you try practising what you preach, for a change?' She rounded on him, acceptance of the fact that she had taken all she possibly could suddenly liberating her—she could say what she liked and to hell with him! 'Though why should you? After all, you're the great Max Bradley, who considers it his God-given right to call all the shots! If you don't think the atmosphere is conducive to your getting your own way—no problem, you'll change it! And what do you plan changing it to this time?' she raged. 'Let's see, you've already tried——'

'Whatever I've tried, I haven't had much success!' he roared, taking a lunging step towards her, then halting abruptly. 'I don't plan changing anything, Abby; I've had enough. I made a bad mistake letting myself get involved with you—but at least I've the guts to admit to my mistakes!'

'Letting yourself get involved with me?' gasped Abby, the words a breathless squeak of indignation. 'You don't "let" yourself become involved with women, Max—you stalk them in the same way as any other predator stalks his quarry, and you do it simply for the sheer hell of it! Just because you didn't succeed with me——'

'I didn't succeed with you, Abby?' he queried, his voice dropping to sudden softness as he stepped towards her. 'If that's the case, what are you still so afraid of?'

'I'm not afraid of you!' she croaked, then, realising that she had begun retreating from him, defiantly stood her ground.

'What, not even of falling in love with me?' he taunted, reaching out and placing his hands lightly on her shoulders.

'That's the last thing I'd be afraid of with you!'

'So what's your problem, Abby?' he growled, his eyes darkly accusing. 'Did I ever deny that I was yours to take? You want me—yet something's always stopped you reaching out and taking me.'

'Stop it!' she protested. 'Stop making it sound as though people were snacks to be grabbed and devoured.'

'I suppose next you'll be claiming you're frightened I'll give you indigestion,' he murmured, drawing her slowly towards him.

'Why do you have to twist everything I say?' she protested hoarsely, battling against the treacherous weakening of her body.

'Why indeed? Especially when it's already so twisted to start with,' he retorted, jerking her fiercely against him.

Clamping her arms to her sides, she resorted to trying to fill her mind with thoughts of vast arctic wastes in an attempt to counteract the potent persuasion of his hotly probing mouth. When those icy wastes began to melt before her mind's eye, she conjured up visions of the waves hurling themselves from the gale-tossed sea on the beach below. But nothing her mind could come up with had the power to distract her from the need burgeoning to savage life from deep within her.

'Don't do this to me,' he groaned against her already succumbing mouth. 'You know you prove nothing to either of us by refusing to put your arms around me... For once, Abby... be honest with me!'

His words made no sense to her, but it was the stark anguish in their plea that demolished the last of her tattered defences. But as her arms rose to cling fiercely around him she knew that she had in fact proved something to herself with her hopeless attempts to resist him—that it was love itself she had been denying with such frantic futility.

The honesty he had demanded was there in the guileless ardency with which her mouth gave itself to his, and in the trembling eagerness of her hands as they caressed and explored against the muscled tautness of his back, and it was there without reservation in the melting acquiescence of her body as it uninhibitedly moulded itself to the searing fire of his.

'Abby!' he groaned, catching her face between his hands and forcibly drawing her head away from his own still torridly searching lips. 'Abby, I...' He broke off, uncertainty and disbelief mingling with the darkness of desire in the eyes boring down into hers. 'There are few who haven't done things they feel ashamed of at some time or other in their lives,' he whispered hoarsely. 'I could tell you of things I've done that you'd probably hate me for, but——'

'No!' she protested, the word exploding from her passionately. No matter what he might have done in the past, her every instinct told her it could never be anything that would warrant her hatred... She loved him too much. She loved him!

'But, Abby——'

'No! Don't dredge up the past...it doesn't matter!' she protested vehemently, turning her head and pressing her lips in a frantic kiss against his palm. She needed to think clearly, but her head was spinning and her heart thudding crazily as she tried to search for a rational reason for his suddenly feeling a compulsion to confess past sins to her and only came up with one that wasn't in the least rational. 'Max——'

They both started at the sound of an ear-splitting crash coming from the garden. Releasing her, he strode towards the back door and switched on the outside light.

'One of the trees in the garden has just lost a branch,' he muttered as he peered out into the night.

Still lost in her own private world of hope and confusion, Abby raced to his side, her still trembling body leaning heavily against his, as though seeking reassurance, as she too peered out.

'I'd better get the cars under cover,' he said, moving so abruptly away from her that she almost lost her balance. He paused as he reached the door, but his back was still to her when he called out, 'You'd better get out of those damp clothes and into bed...it's late.'

A silence, eerie and oppressive, descended around her when she heard the front door slam behind him, only to be broken a few seconds later by the muffled sound of the car's engine.

She loved him, she thought dazedly...and he had wanted to confess his past sins to her, as an eager, unsophisticated first-time lover might have done...yet all she felt was a strange, almost premonitory uneasiness.

One minute she had been in his arms, and then he had gone. It was almost as though he had welcomed the distraction that had separated them...and his previous lack of any apparent concern over what was obviously an exceedingly expensive car had always horrified her.

But he had felt that urge to confess... and he had expressed concern over her damp clothes...

She gave a soft groan of understanding, then raced from the kitchen, up the stairs and into her room.

What heat permeated up from the kitchen range only served to take the ice from the chill in the room, but tonight she had her own fire burning within her as she undressed and sped to the unwelcoming bathroom. And though that fire was still raging inside her when she at last got into her bed, she lay shivering and uncertain beneath the duvet.

It was different when she was in his arms, she thought nervously, whereas lying here and cold-bloodedly waiting for him to come to her was another matter altogether.

He would come to her and they would make love, she told herself determinedly, and once she was back in his arms everything would be all right because she would have love to guide her. For several seconds she lay there with that thought enshrined in her mind; then she gave a groan of despair and buried her head under the duvet.

She tried reasoning with herself, but it took long minutes of frantic soul-searching before she accepted the fact that to save them both considerable, and unnecessary, embarrassment she would have to find the words to tell him of her complete lack of sexual experience the instant he came to her.

Though reaching that decision went some way to ease the stifling apprehension that had gripped her, it returned, magnified tenfold, the instant she heard his tread on the stairs. A few minutes later it was the sound of a bath being run that left her mind reeling in a devastation of total confusion.

By the time she had given up trying to convince herself that it was her own ignorance in such matters that was reducing her to this mindless state, he had taken his bath and had long since returned to his room... and she was incapable of forming a single coherent thought.

Perhaps he had sensed her inexperience and hadn't wanted to rush her, she reasoned in a last-ditch attempt to cling on to her dreams. Or perhaps pigs could fly, she contradicted an instant later, while tears of hurt and bewilderment coursed silently down her cheeks.

Now all she craved was the merciful oblivion of sleep, even as she despaired of ever achieving it. On other nights she had managed to set aside whatever trials had beset her during the day, lulled by the rhythmic lapping of the waves against the shore. But tonight the restless seething of the sea only complemented her own inner turmoil, encouraging and condoning it.

From almost the first moment their paths had crossed he had had the power to unsettle her, magnetising her, rejecting her, one moment wilfully awakening needs in her such as she had never dreamed of possessing, the next spurning her with icy contempt. There had been so many warning signals, none of which she had heeded; her premonitions, inexplicable and disturbingly primitive though they had once seemed, had been too powerful for her to have relegated them to the recesses of her mind as she had. She had allowed herself to become lost under layer after layer of doubt and confusion... and it was in that terrible state, where she was barely capable of distinguishing up from down, that she had come to love him. Once she had passionately believed love to be synonymous with happiness, yet now she could only equate it with misery and confusion.

She sat up in bed with a start, roused from her torpor of half-sleep by a sudden noise that subsided to a grating, creaking sound, then swelled to a loud clatter.

She listened as the noise persisted, the alarmed thud of her heart accelerating out of control when she heard the door of Max's room open and close and his swift tread on the stairs.

Feeling heavy-limbed and exhausted, she struggled into her dressing-gown, her teeth chattering with the cold as she went to the window and looked out.

The outside light flooded into the inky darkness almost as she arrived at the window, but she drew hurriedly back from it when Max's tall, familiar figure stepped back from the house and peered up at its façade. Then he moved back towards the house, to where one of the shutters had come loose, and, as she watched him secure it, she felt herself shiver as she saw the ferocity with which the wind was attacking him. It tore around his body in rampant fury, creating chaos as it whipped through the glossy thickness of his hair, tugging at the bulky darkness of his sweat-shirt then plastering it like a second skin against his braced body.

She let out a groan of horror when the second shutter tore free and he moved towards it, coming much more clearly into her sight. His feet were bare and, apart from the couple of inches of white boxer shorts beneath his sweatshirt, his long, athlete's legs were completely unprotected against the savage force of the wind.

She turned from the window and sagged against the wall in weary disbelief. She had been standing there fretting over him as though he had been a helpless child, rather than the strapping specimen of manhood he was. She was completely and utterly out of her senses!

Of course she was, she told herself with a resignation tinged with fear as she made her way back to the bed. She loved him, didn't she? The fact that she hadn't chosen to, that he was the last man she would have picked had she ever had a choice, was immaterial...she loved him!

She sat down on the edge of the bed, wondering when what she was at last admitting to herself would really hit her—and what the effect would be on her. Then suddenly she was hearing not words but the anguished pleading that had been in his tone earlier.

'Max,' she whispered brokenly, then froze as something crashed down on the roof, then bounced and rolled its way down its slope. She heard his cry in a breathless instant of quiet before whatever had fallen hit the ground. 'Max!' she screamed in anguished terror, racing from the room and hurling herself down the stairs.

His name was a choked sob trapped inside her as she tore open the back door and flew to where he had been standing. Strewn all around were shards of pottery, but Max was nowhere in sight.

'Abby, for God's sake get back!' he called, appearing from round the side of the house and racing to her side. 'It might not be safe here,' he said, grabbing hold of her and hauling her away to the safety of the lawn. 'The cowl was blown off the chimney and for all I know more could come down.'

She barely heard what he was saying as she flung herself against him in an orgy of relief and a desperate need to ascertain for herself that he was truly unharmed.

'I thought it had fallen on you,' she choked, her hands uncoordinated as they tested and prodded, moving from his chest to his shoulders, pausing to check they were both intact before rising to cup his face in their trembling caress.

'Abby,' he protested hoarsely, bewilderment softening his features. 'I'm perfectly all right.'

'But if it had fallen on your head... you could have been killed,' she sobbed, her fingers sinking into the tousled darkness of his hair as though fearful of finding he had lied.

'Abby, what on earth's got into you? I tell you...' His words petered to a shuddering groan as he dragged her into his arms and crushed her to him.

She heard him groan her name as he buried his face against her windswept hair and felt the powerful surge of desire with which his body responded to the spontaneous invitation of hers.

'We'll be blown away and out to sea,' he protested unsteadily as the wind shrieked past their locked bodies, but his arms only tightened and his mouth returned to its passionate exploration of hers.

It was the blatant urgency with which his body inflamed hers that drove her to a point almost beyond endurance, but it was the soft, incoherently murmured endearments with which he interspersed the frenzied ardour of his kisses that lost her to him forever. And when he lifted her high in his arms and carried her through the house the newest and most intense of the wild sensations bombarding her was that of unbridled hope.

CHAPTER NINE

THERE had been a provocative gentleness in his hands as they had slowly stripped her, then guided her down on to the bed. It was only when he joined her, drawing her intoxicated body to the naked fire of his, that she sensed the intensely volatile nature of the passion simmering beneath that surface gentleness. It was a recognition that, far from frightening her, filled her with reckless exhilaration, and it was with the abandonment born of complete inexperience that her body responded to his as though being challenged to strip from him those last tenuous restraints holding him back. And it was a challenge she confronted fearlessly and without the thought ever occurring to her of any possibility of danger in what she might unleash in him.

'No!' he protested, having to resort to using force just to turn her slightly from him and even then having to use the superior strength of his limbs to keep her there. 'You're rushing things... and I want you to want me as you've wanted no other man before,' he whispered passionately.

His words stirred a memory in her of what she had intended telling him, but it was then that he began running his hands over her body in a slow, sensuous caress, and the memory was lost to her.

'Am I asking too much of you?' he groaned, his hands and his mouth on her, teasing and tormenting her till there was no part of her free from the need threatening to tear her apart. 'Am I, Abby?'

She shook her head, the madness possessing her making speech impossible. And she cried out in an agony of impatience as she felt the soft breath of his laughter against her skin. But it was when she stopped fighting him, entwining her arms pleadingly around his neck and sobbing his name, that his laughter deteriorated into husky, incoherent murmurings that were still sweetly bathing her ears when her body received the explosive power of his.

For one hovering moment of timelessness it was as though she had witnessed her past life end and her future begin, a consciousness she had barely assimilated before her every sense was being jarred to rapturous life, the melting beneath the onslaught of an almost unbearable pleasure. And when, before she could begin to recover from it, that indescribable pleasure reared up and overwhelmed her once again, her bemused cries of protest and delight were answered by the rumbling ardour of his own.

There came a time when the breathless softness of his endearments took on a new, harsher urgency, goading her to impossibly new heights with the savage intensity of a need which she felt must explode if it wasn't to drive her reason from her completely. And when that shattering moment finally came, it was as though love had been detonated between them and it was love that came bursting from her in her dazed, incoherent cries of joy.

For a long while they lay entwined and spent in each other's arms, neither of them uttering a word. It was Abby who finally broke the silence, just a single, lazily murmured word of protest when he slipped from her arms.

'But if I don't find the quilt,' he chuckled softly, 'we could well end up with frost-bite.' Having retrieved the duvet from where it had fallen to the floor, he placed it over them and returned to her side. 'I told you we should have left both beds in this room,' he grumbled huskily, his chin nuzzling against her head.

'I'd still want you in this one, even if there were two of them in here,' she murmured contentedly, still floating a long way from reality.

'At least we could have pushed them together and had a decent-sized bed,' he argued lazily. 'And besides, that quilt I practically had to scour Cornwall to find is goosedown and twice the size of this minute, lightweight effort of yours.'

'What possessed you to get a double quilt for a single bed?' she enquired, her words breathlessly groggy.

'Because I happen to be a big lad and single beds and I weren't meant for each other—as you'll no doubt discover for yourself before this night is through.'

'Having a large quilt isn't going to make the bed any bigger,' muttered Abby, beginning to feel slightly puzzled.

'I know it isn't...but they only had double ones in the shop.'

She nodded, but said nothing. Now that she had started returning to earth, the fact that their conversation was centred around the size of his continental quilt was beginning to strike her as more than a little odd.

'Abby?' he queried, tugging gently on her hair.

'Yes?'

'I was just checking that you hadn't nodded off on me.'

'I haven't.' She completed her return to reality with a dismal thud. He sounded so matter-of-fact...so cheerful!

Perhaps that incredible magic they had just shared had been no more than a figment of her imagination, she thought miserably as all the old doubts and confusions began hammering on the doors of her mind. 'I was thinking,' she said, a challenge in her words.

'I see,' he muttered, plainly not in the least interested in meeting that challenge.

'Yes,' she stated. They were lying naked in one another's arms, having just made love, she thought incredulously, yet he was determinedly avoiding making any reference to the fact. 'I was thinking how strange it is that one moment two people can be baring their souls to one another with a total lack of inhibition, while the next have nothing better to do than discuss duvet sizes.'

Her heart plummeted when he removed his arms from around her and lay beside her with his hands linked behind his head.

'And you bared your soul to me, did you, Abby?' he asked grimly.

'I was merely telling you the thoughts going through my mind,' she said, thoroughly disorientated by the pain of her hurt and disbelief.

'Tell me, Abby, what sort of post-coital conversations do you usually indulge in?'

She sat bolt upright in horror and consternation.

'I...I thought you'd have realised!' she choked before the thought staggered into her reeling mind that there was probably no reason why he should have. 'But I don't care whether you did or not—you're a cold-hearted monster!' she cried out, devastated and fighting him with every ounce of her strength as he tried to take her in his arms.

'That's what I'll probably end up as before you're through with me,' he accused harshly, forcing her down and imprisoning her against him. 'Abby, of course I realised,' he groaned. 'I can't even say why, exactly...but I wouldn't have believed you had you tried denying it.'

'Why on earth would I try denying it?' she gasped, her now half-hearted attempts to escape faltering as her body responded with a violence of excitement to the enveloping closeness of his. 'Max, why do you always give the impression you think I'm incapable of uttering a single honest word?'

'I...it's just that some people lie outright and others do so by omission,' he muttered, his body responding with equal ardour to hers. 'To say I think you're incapable of uttering——'

'Max, I'd prefer a conversation about duvets to this tortuous rigmarole,' she protested miserably, convinced her mind had deserted her.

'Abby, why can't you be less inflexible?' he pleaded, his hands moving compulsively over her body. 'We all have definite views on matters...but there are times when we're forced to accommodate those of others, to a certain extent, otherwise...oh, hell, Abby, do you really want to return to the subject of duvets?'

'Perhaps you'd feel happier if I went and got you your own precious duvet,' she murmured, accepting that she had most definitely lost her mind as laughter began bubbling up from within her.

'No,' he growled, his mouth roaming in hot, frenzied kisses against her face. 'I want you at least to attempt to understand... Abby, you've given me proof that you want me as you've never wanted any other man, simply through my being the first,' he sighed. 'But what proof have I to give you that I've never wanted any woman as I do you? All I can offer is my word.'

The stark desolation in his words tore into her heart, heightening her own desolation at the knowledge that their minds simply didn't work on the same plane . . . To ask her to understand him was asking the impossible.

But where their minds were forced to stumble through the minefield of their innate differences, their bodies once again fused in the glorious harmony of absolute understanding.

It took it some while for it to sink in with Abby that the voices drifting up to her from below must have something to do with the workmen and that Max must have let them into the house.

She sat up in bed and gazed around her, the last traces of the drowsy blankness of sleep blasted from her mind by the searing intrusion of the memories assailing her.

She leapt from the bed, a ruthlessly detached part of her pointing out that there was something vaguely unnatural—unwholesome, almost—in the way she was throwing herself into getting bathed and dressed as though getting down to the workmen who had arrived so unexpectedly early was the only consideration in her life.

The folly of her ostrich-like refusal to pause and take stock of herself hit her the instant she entered the kitchen. There were three men in the room, two of whom might as well not have existed once her eyes had sought out the tall figure at the sink engrossed in pouring water into a coffee jug, the man in whose arms, her every jangling sense was reminding her, she had spent the long hours of the night.

'Mr Bodrigan,' she said, forcing her attention to the older and taller of the two men by the range.

'Jim,' smiled the man she had chosen as her site foreman. 'I've brought my son Harry along to give us a hand,' he added, while the young man beside him greeted her with a cheery grin. 'I was just explaining to Mr Bradley——'

'Max,' corrected the man still absorbed in his coffee-making.

Jim Bodrigan's smile broadened. 'I was just explaining to Max that I thought it best if we brought what heavy equipment we'll be needing in today. If this rain keeps up we could run into access problems with the road.'

'Is there any danger of the work being held up?' asked Abby, the effort it was taking to concentrate alarming her.

'No—not if we get started right away. And if the worst comes to the worst, I've a four-wheel-drive vehicle I can arrange to have the men picked up and brought here in. I'm sorry to be rearranging your schedule like this...'

'I'm most grateful that you have,' exclaimed Abby, worried in case she had given the wrong impression with what must be her noticeable edginess. Jim Bodrigan's quick-thinking initiative only served to show her how invaluable he would be to her—the last thing she wanted was to offend him in the slightest. 'And I'm only glad I've got myself such a good foreman,' she added earnestly.

Jim flashed her an almost paternal grin. 'Another thing I was saying to Max was that I wouldn't risk either the Renault or the Aston Martin on that road if this rain continues for too much longer. Anyway, to get back to business... there's plenty of shed space for storage.'

As he briskly ran through his plans, and even though only part of her attention was on him, Abby could see all too clearly why Jim Bodrigan's name was on the esteemed Bradley list. The rest of her attention was centred entirely on the man who had at last started pouring the coffee, the making of which had kept him so abnormally engrossed for so long.

It wasn't as though she had expected him to come bounding ecstatically over to her, she thought bitterly...but he hadn't even greeted her, hadn't cast so much as a glance in her direction!

Jim had proceeded to the subject of taking delivery of the kitchen equipment when Max turned to hand a cup of coffee to Abby, facing her for the first time since she had entered the room.

She had got to a stage of simply not knowing what to expect when their eyes finally met, but the flash of raw hunger she encountered knocked the breath from her lungs and brought the stain of scarlet to her cheeks as she reached out a noticeably trembling hand to receive the cup.

She must have expected something, she thought numbly, otherwise she wouldn't have been so completely thrown by what she had seen. But there had been something terribly wrong about that look in his eyes... It had been such a burningly predatory look and one lacking any hint of the tenderness that surely there should be between lovers. She closed her eyes momentarily, only to find vivid memories flooding her and threatening to suffocate her with their hot sweetness. There had never been anything but confusion and contention between them and she was a fool to have expected anything to have changed, she told herself with a stomach-churning bitterness as she forced herself to join the men by the window where Jim was spreading out a copy of her plans.

* * *

'I honestly think it's about time you gave some thought to getting those cars out of here,' stated Jim several hours later. 'Harry and I will take a lunch-break and pick up some more gear after.' He turned to Abby. 'I don't think there's anything else you can do here today, Abby. Once the men have got started in the morning, I'll send someone to the hotel for you and Max—there's no point in risking bringing one of your cars down, even if the rain has let up.'

Abby smiled as she nodded.

'That sounds fine,' said Max. 'Except that I shan't be around to be picked up in the morning—I'm returning to London later on today.'

'I'll get my things together,' said Abby before anyone else had a chance to say anything, though she wasn't in the least certain how she managed to produce the words.

Having to force herself not to break into a run, she left the room and climbed the stairs. By the time she reached her room her legs were like jelly and her breath was coming in short, agonised gasps.

At first she leaned weakly against the closed door, gulping in air and willing herself to believe that this wasn't happening to her, that none of this had happened to her. Oh, but it had, she almost cried out aloud . . . and now she was being given a taste of how cold-blooded sophisticates went about their sordid affairs—ending them with an abrupt dismissal via a complete stranger. Except that theirs hadn't even been what could be called an affair, she reminded herself with savage hurt—a one-night stand was about the only description it warranted!

Biting back the tears she would rather have died than shed, she tore around the room, gathering up the few of her things not stored in her case and hurling them into it. Then she started stripping the bed, holding her breath as she fought to ignore the indefinable scent of him that reached out to her as she gathered up the bedclothes and rammed them into the bag in which she had brought them.

It was as she retrieved the pillow from where it had fallen to the floor that her control deserted her and she hugged the pillow to her, burying her face against it and sobbing as though her heart would break as the scent of him overpowered her and the memory of his voice filled her ears in passionate caress.

Gullible beyond belief though she was, it was her own over-inflated pride that had contributed most to her downfall, she accused herself bitterly. He had read her like a book and thrown down the challenge he had known she would be too stupid to resist.

She flung the pillow angrily from her—talk about taking candy from a baby! From the start he had played her like an expert angler, arrogantly letting her know what it was he wanted from her, then unhurriedly setting his trap. Calculatingly offering her just enough veiled hints to raise her pathetic hopes whenever she had shown signs of having been pushed too far, he had gradually tied her up in the most excruciating of mental knots until a time had come when all he had had to do was crook his little finger and she was his. And this was the cold-blooded manipulator on whom she had squandered the precious gift of love!

She scrubbed with angry contempt at the tears already drying on her cheeks, then gathered her things together. Yes, she had been used in the most despicable manner by a man who hadn't even the grace to give her the time of day once he had had his way. But there was one thing she was blessed with, even if it had deserted her at a time when she had most needed it, and that was common sense—and it was her common sense that offered her a crumb of comfort from the knowledge that it would have taken a woman of a strength she simply didn't possess to have survived unscathed once Max Bradley had her in his callously predatory sights.

Without actually creeping down the stairs and out of the house, she made her escape as quietly as she possibly could. Once she had loaded up the car she returned to the front door.

'I'm off now—see you in the morning, Jim!'

She closed the door and hurried back to her car.

'Please, Reggie, don't let me down!' she wailed in desperation as the engine responded to her attempt to start with a lethargic cough. 'There's a good lad!' she exclaimed with relief when the engine at last chugged protestingly to life.

It was only when she was about to ease out into the road that she gave a backward look towards the house, then groaned in consternation as she spotted the Aston Martin reversing into sight from the back of the house.

'This is all I need!' she protested weakly, putting her foot down and instantly feeling her wheels spin as she turned into the mud-washed road.

When she looked in her mirror again, the Aston Martin was right on her tail, its pristine bodywork rapidly disappearing beneath the mud being thrown up by her spinning tyres. She gave a shriek of horrified disbelief as the car behind thudded straight into the back of hers, and had barely lowered her window to protest when she felt the impact of a second hit.

'What the hell do you think you're doing?' she shrieked, almost beside herself with fright and fury.

'I'm trying to shift you!' he roared back, leaning his head through his opened window. 'Damn it, Abby, stop giving it so much throttle!'

Soon he would be gone and this nightmare would be behind her, she tried comforting herself once the nerve-racking shunting had ended and her tyres were gingerly gripping the road surface. No, she contradicted herself with fatalistic grimness, the nightmare of having him around might be over, but that of loving a man she should only despise would always be with her.

Unnerved by the presence of the powerful car still hugging her tail, and with the rain suddenly coming down in buckets once again, making visibility scarily patchy, she knew she was dangerously close to absolute breaking-point. And it was then, as a sense of utter helplessness began crowding in on her, that his voice began filling her head: soft words of passion, words that sometimes pleaded, sometimes beguiled, but words always filled with a treacherous promise of love.

If she was going to disintegrate over a man, she accused herself harshly, her spirit rearing up in protest, the least she could have done was choose one worthy of doing so over!

He had pulled up beside her and was stepping from his car as she raced towards the doors of the hotel.

Her acute awareness of his smouldering presence beside her had the humiliating effect of distracting her from what she was trying to say as she booked her room.

'And what about you, Mr Bradley?' enquired the proprietress, turning to Max with the sort of smile she plainly kept in reserve for the chosen few.

'I'm afraid it's back to London for me,' replied Max, his smile, if anything, outdoing hers. 'But if you could rustle us up a table for lunch, I'd be most grateful.'

It was on the tip of Abby's tongue to inform him he would be lunching alone, but something beyond her control made her bite back the words... She might be eager to see the back of him, but her tattered pride needed something to boost it on its long road towards restoration. She would have lunch with him all right, she decided recklessly, and even if it killed her she would do everything in her power to ensure that he left with the impression that last night had meant as little to her as it obviously had to him.

'I'll just get my things from the car,' she told the proprietress.

'No, don't you worry about that, Miss Grantham; I'll send someone out for them,' replied the woman, waving a hand in the direction of the dining-room. 'You go and enjoy your lunch.'

'This is a surprise,' muttered Max, as a waiter led them to a window table in the deserted dining-room, 'your deigning to have lunch with me.'

'I can't think why,' replied Abby with studied indifference, taking her seat.

'Perhaps I'm being ultra-sensitive,' he drawled, glancing at the menu, then tossing it aside, 'but your departure seemed a little abrupt—to say the least.'

'You're right—you are being ultra-sensitive,' replied Abby, the thought crossing her mind that most people had more sensitivity in their toenails than he had in his entire body. 'And as for having lunch with you, how could I possibly pass up this last opportunity of having you guide me through the finer points of a menu?'

The look he gave her expressed his reaction to that remark far more eloquently than any words could have.

'I'll have a plain omelette and a green salad,' he informed the waiter, then turned towards the window and gazed morosely out at the sea.

'I'll have the same,' said Abby, the very idea of food making her feel suddenly queasy. 'Max, I'd like this meal to be on me,' she exclaimed, desperate for distraction as her queasiness showed signs of blossoming into full-blown nausea. 'And I thought it would be nice to have a bottle of champagne or something with it.'

Well, at least that was one way of getting his attention, she thought as he swivelled round to face her, his expression one of unguarded astonishment.

'I don't drink and drive,' he retorted coldly, his expression reverting to one of indifference as he regained control of himself. 'And besides, I wasn't aware we had anything to celebrate.'

'Perhaps you don't, Max,' she replied, her words controlled despite the fact she had just discovered that, contrary to what she had always thought, she actually would be capable of physical violence. 'But I do—in fact, I've rather a lot to celebrate.'

'Really?' he drawled. 'Well, perhaps you'd care to enlighten me as to what it is.'

'I doubt if I could do that,' she murmured, apprehension slowly creeping through her. 'It's something rather private—and nothing that need concern you in the least.'

She should have had more sense than to get herself embroiled in something like this, she told herself frantically. She wasn't used to playing this sort of game—one likely to prove exceedingly dangerous, given the expertise of the man with whom she had so foolishly elected to play it.

'Abby, if you're trying to tell me something, I suggest you get on with it,' he snapped before resuming his scowling inspection of the sea. 'I don't happen to be in the mood for tortuous games.'

'How unusual,' she retorted, limp from the effort of having to contain her mounting rage. 'I always thought that the more tortuous and devious the game the better you enjoyed it.'

'Did you, indeed?' he snapped, glowering across the table at her with tight-lipped fury as the waiter arrived and served their food.

'Yes,' flung back Abby, the instant the waiter had left. 'But I obviously should have realised that would only apply to games instigated by you!'

'Tell me, Abby,' he enquired with menacing softness, 'where does the game we played last night fit into all this?'

Unable to think of any other way to gain the time she so desperately needed in which to struggle for a scrap of composure, Abby rammed a forkful of her omelette into her mouth and prayed she wouldn't choke. It was her pride that had so blindly driven her into this encounter, and the price Max would extract would be the total annihilation of that pride—of that she had no doubt.

'Abby, I asked you a question,' he pointed out in that same menacingly soft tone.

'But not a very wise one,' she heard herself reply in an unnaturally controlled voice. 'I really don't think you'd like the answer.'

'Try me!' he snarled, flinging down the fork which had never once touched his food.

'Just who the hell do you think you are, Max?' she exploded, panic running riot in her with the sudden vision of his taking her by the throat and trying to throttle an answer from her. She had trotted out defensive, meaningless words in an effort to salvage the pride he would any second destroy beyond repair—and now she was being called on to give meaning to their nonsense! 'You consider it your God-given right to play your contemptible games with any woman unfortunate enough to catch your eye! But your trouble is that you simply can't take it when a woman retaliates and beats you at your own game!'

'You're claiming to have beaten me at my own game, are you?' he snarled, half rising to his feet. 'You're...' He broke off and slumped back down on his chair, his words dropping to a dazed, husky whisper as he continued. 'Abby, how can you talk in terms of games? You were a virgin, for God's sake!'

And she loved him, she cried in silent despair, a terrible lethargy spreading within her as she wondered how he could possibly have been so blind as not to have seen the love staring him so openly in the face. It was the realisation that nobody could have been that blind, and that any moment now he would be throwing that love back in her face as he coldly went in for the kill, that hardened her resolve and brought a cynical travesty of a laugh from her.

'Yes, I was a virgin,' she replied, defiance in her eyes as they met his, 'but I wouldn't set too much store by that, if I were you, Max.'

She had never understood him, always been confused by him, but never more so than in that moment when she witnessed the succession of negative expressions chasing one another across his completely unguarded face in the instant before he leapt to his feet with a bellow of rage, kicking his chair aside before striding from the room.

CHAPTER TEN

'ABBY, instead of trekking all the way back to Kingston, why don't you come back to my place after work and we can go round to Jennifer's together?' Julie had suggested.

And it was probably just as well she had, thought Abby as she lay back in the bath at Julie's flat after a particularly exhausting day, otherwise she might have been tempted to ring Jennifer and put off this evening.

'Pop round on Friday evening for a bite of supper,' Jennifer had said. 'Julie's coming and as Paul's out with a client the three of us could have a good old natter—something I find I'm missing now that I'm in the office so rarely. And besides, I want to hear all about your trip to Canada and the wedding.'

Yes, she decided, had she not accepted Julie's invitation to leave from here, she might well have cried off... In fact, from the moment she had awoken, she had been jittery and completely out of sorts.

She gave a sudden, violent shake of her head, then climbed out of the bath. She had to stop doing this to herself! Damage limitation—that was what survival was all about, she informed herself angrily as she towelled herself dry. And whatever other damage he had done her, she wasn't about to let the spectre of Max Bradley impair her relationship with his sister.

She wrapped the towel around her and sat down on the bath mat, leaning back against the side of the bath in frowning concentration.

At least she had reached a stage when she had given up kidding herself a miracle would happen and she would be cured of him—though the fact that hearing his name no longer resulted in her throwing a complete internal wobbly was probably something of a miracle in itself, she admitted dejectedly. But it was stark pain that haunted her face as she thought back to those agonising days in Cornwall without him and remembered the terror she had felt when the full extent of her own devastation had hit her. Somehow or other she had not only survived but had completed the job without a hitch, only to be thrown in the path of her next impossible hurdle—Canada. Using jet lag as her crutch, she had hobbled through both Christmas and Elaine's wedding without raising any suspicions in her blissfully distracted sister.

Her return to work had been another hurdle, but one she had limped over with less effort than she might have anticipated.

She rose and went to Julie's bedroom to get dressed and, though her mind still churned, it was with positive rather than negative thoughts that it did so.

The truth was that there would be no miracle and she would probably never return to being the person she had once been, but she *was* on the road to recovery and it was a road on which she intended to stay.

'That's better!' Julie greeted her, as Abby entered the living-room. 'You were looking whacked earlier. What were you doing today—bricklaying?'

'As near as,' laughed Abby, sinking down on to a roomy armchair. 'But thanks a million for letting me bath and change here—I honestly don't think I'd have been able to face driving back into London if I'd had to go home first.'

'For heaven's sake, I've been inviting you round here ever since I moved in.' Julie grinned, pouring some tea and handing her a cup. 'So get that down you and tell me all about Christmas in Canada. You've been back over two weeks now and I still haven't had a chance to hear it all.'

'Well, you'll just have to wait,' laughed Abby, 'because Jennifer wants to hear about it and I'm not going over it all twice.'

'I remember now,' exclaimed Julie. 'Jennifer did mention something about Paul being involved with your sister at one time... quite a coincidence, really.'

'I suppose it was,' replied Abby non-committally, gazing down at her cup.

'Well, it'll be nice just the three of us getting together for a good old natter,' said Julie. 'I think that's one of the things Jennifer's missing now that she's only coming into the office when we're really stretched. It's a shame I'll have to leave fairly early, but Andrew's plane gets in just after ten.'

'Who are you kidding it's a shame?' teased Abby. Andrew Croft was an airline pilot to whom Julie had recently become engaged and whose flight schedules had become the most important consideration in her life.

'You wait till you meet the man of your dreams, my girl,' warned Julie with a chuckle, then glanced at her watch. 'It's about time we made a move.'

'I'll just get my things,' said Abby, relieved to be on the move. She had already met the man of her dreams, only to find her dreams had become a nightmare. 'It's probably best if I follow you there in my car, then you can go straight to the airport from Jennifer's.'

* * *

'Have you met Andrew yet?' asked Jennifer, rejoining Abby on the sofa before the fire after having seen Julie off.

'Only very briefly, when he picked her up from the office once. He seemed very likeable.'

'He is—he's a darling of a man,' agreed Jennifer enthusiastically. 'And he and Julie are absolutely right for each other.' She glanced down at the photographs that Abby had brought of the wedding and which lay strewn between them. 'And what about Elaine and Rob—did you have good feelings about your sister's choice?'

'Oh, I did,' exclaimed Abby. She had been so wrapped up in her own heartache that it hadn't been until she was about to come face to face with the man who was so soon to become her brother-in-law that the possibility of her sister having made a mistake actually crossed her mind. 'It suddenly hit me just before I met him that I'd know if he wasn't right for her and that there would be nothing I could do about it.'

'I know exactly what you mean,' sympathised Jennifer. 'I'm never certain whether it's a curse or a blessing, but there are times when I have exactly that sort of sixth sense—and it's invariably right. So Rob passed the test, did he?' she finished with a chuckle.

'With flying colours,' declared Abby. 'He's a lovely, warm and incredibly gentle bear of a man.'

'And gorgeous with it,' declared Jennifer, gazing down at one of the photographs she had tidied into a pile. Then she lifted her head, her expression altering markedly. 'I'm not too sure how to go about this,' she sighed, 'but it's about time I gave you the apology I owe you.'

Abby gave her a startled look. 'What apology?'

'The one you're owed over my getting myself into the most dreadful muddle...and letting it colour my attitude towards you during my brief period of lunacy,' she replied, then added in a burst, 'When Paul and I first met he was completely honest with me about his relationship with your sister.'

'And he was equally as honest with Elaine,' said Abby. 'Paul is one of the most decent men there is.'

'Abby, I felt desperately sorry for Elaine—loving him as I did, even having known him for so short a time, I could imagine how I would feel if I were to lose him. But I never felt any guilt.'

'And neither should you have,' said Abby firmly. 'Not that I'd ever have understood that until recently, when Elaine made me face the real facts,' she added with a sigh.

'I'm sure if it had been the other way round it would have taken a great deal of ramming down my volatile brother's throat—I dread to think how he'd have reacted,' said Jennifer. 'But that's the way most of us tend to react when we see someone we love being hurt.'

Abby gazed into the fire, the sense of a terrible loss aching sharply through her as words Max had once uttered returned to her: '...I love my sister, and God help anyone who does anything to hurt her while I still have breath in my body!'

It was that sort of uncompromising love she had cried out for from him, in her heart of hearts always knowing it was a love that would never be hers.

'I still have difficulty working out exactly what happened,' continued Jennifer. 'Paul says it's because I'd got so run down just before I became pregnant—he and Max had been nagging me to take some time off to recuperate. But I was on such a delirious high once I knew about the baby—heavens, I could have taken on the Houses of Parliament single-handed and still floated! Then I hit earth with the most horrible thud.'

'How do you mean?' asked Abby, her perplexed look bringing one of almost exasperated affection to her companion's lovely face.

'Abby, my love, not only do you not appear to hold any grudge against me for the appalling way I behaved towards you,' she sighed, 'but you also appear oblivious of there being any grounds for you bearing me one.'

'But there aren't any,' protested Abby. 'All right, so there was a time when I felt you were being rather cool towards me, but that was at a stage when I'd got it into my head that working for you was some sort of disloyalty to Elaine—so I was hardly reasoning logically at the time. And besides, I wasn't the only person worried about you—everyone was. By the time you told us about the baby, you were back to your old self... Jennifer, there's not the slightest reason why I should bear you a grudge, for heaven's sake!'

'Abby, you're sweet-natured almost to a fault—which makes me feel a hundred times worse over my behaviour,' groaned Jennifer. 'For a while I made you the scapegoat for all my imagined woes. I even tried to think up an excuse to fire you—not that the others would have let me get away with it.'

'But...but why?' croaked Abby, unable to believe her ears.

'Because I must have been close to being out of my tiny mind.' Jennifer sighed. 'How else would you describe someone who gets it into her head that there's too much happiness in her life and it can't possibly last? It all sounds so crazy now, but it was almost as though I was set on proving it couldn't last.'

'But what had that to do with me?' asked Abby in a dazed voice.

'You're Elaine's sister and the coincidence of your coming to work for me suddenly seemed laden with significance. Out of the blue I became riddled with guilt over having taken Paul from Elaine... I convinced myself that my happiness had been built on her misery. I saw how upset Paul was when you refused to have anything to do with him and that was when I really started fantasising—telling myself that he was tormented by the same guilts as I was.'

'Paul adores you,' protested Abby. 'It would have been an absolute disaster if he and Elaine——'

'Abby, I know all that—I've always known it, except for that while when my mind simply freaked out on me.'

'Triggered off by my petty-minded nastiness in refusing to speak to Paul,' concluded Abby miserably.

'Oh, no—don't you dare start any of that with me!' wailed Jennifer. 'Abby, the state I was in then, if you'd been friendly towards him I'd probably have got it into my head you were trying to lure him back to Elaine—or something equally far-fetched!' She shook her head, the expression in her eyes touching a sudden chord in Abby and bringing a painful tightness to her chest. 'How about if we just drop this horrible subject altogether?'

'I just might be tempted to bear you a grudge if we don't,' joked Abby, but the uncanny familiarity of her companion's relieved grin was already giving another twist to the knife embedded in her heart.

'One thing I've been meaning to tell you,' exclaimed Jennifer, 'is that Paul and I went down to Max's cottage at the weekend—Abby, you've done a wonderful job on it! I cast a completely detached professional eye over the entire place and was most impressed.'

'I... I'm so glad you liked it,' stammered Abby, painfully conscious of the colour leaping to her cheeks.

'Like it? Abby, it's exactly as I would have envisaged it.' She frowned, plainly puzzled by Abby's reaction, then she flung her hands in the air in a gesture of pure exasperation. 'My God, one of these days I'll swing for that wretched brother of mine!' she groaned. 'Abby, whatever Max says, and the fact that he hasn't bothered to go near the place since it was completed, doesn't matter one jot! His black moods are mercifully rare, but when he's in one nothing on this earth can please him, so you mustn't think it's any reflection of his views on what you've done with the cottage.'

'I... I don't,' floundered Abby, the reserves she had time and again dug into during the past weeks now apparently spent. 'I know Max liked the plans.'

'Oh,' said Jennifer, for a moment nonplussed. For several seconds her candid blue eyes remained trained on Abby, then clouded before her gaze dropped to her lap. 'Oh, hell,' she groaned softly to herself. 'It's understandable that I'd be the last person you'd want to talk to about it.'

'There isn't anything to talk about,' exclaimed Abby far too quickly, an edge of desperation in her words.

'Abby, are you quite sure?' sighed Jennifer. 'Because I'm not. When I say that moods such as the one Max appears to have been in for some time now are rare I mean that they are exceedingly rare. He has an often infuriating knack of letting very little get to him... but I'd say something has definitely been getting to him of late.'

'I really wouldn't know,' muttered Abby, her frozen mind incapable of coming up with anything else.

'But I would,' exclaimed Jennifer. 'I've only seen the man twice since Paul and I got back—and that's most unlike him. And on both those occasions he's flitted in and then out practically before we've had a chance to say more than "hello"—and that's even more unlike him. I don't even know where he spent Christmas... I can't make him out any more.'

Almost transfixed by her overwhelming sense of discomfort, Abby said nothing... There was nothing she could say that wouldn't open up her still gaping wounds beyond endurance.

'Abby, love, I...' Jennifer broke off and their heads both turned towards the door as it opened and Paul walked in.

'Darling, I didn't hear you get back!' exclaimed Jennifer, her face lighting up as she stretched out over the back of the sofa towards him.

'I must be losing track of which day is which,' exclaimed Paul, stooping to kiss his wife. 'I'd clean forgotten it was tonight Abby was coming round. Hello, Abby.' He grinned, reaching over and ruffling her hair. 'Unfortunately I got dragged into a working dinner.'

'You've been working too hard,' complained his wife, smiling up at him as he walked round and seated himself between them on the sofa.

'Not any more,' he promised. 'We got it all sewn up tonight. So—let's have a look at the photographs,' he said, slipping an arm round each of them. 'You have brought some, haven't you, Abby?'

'Of course she has,' laughed Jennifer, producing them. 'And they're... good heavens, Max.'

Paul gave a groaning laugh. 'I clean forgot,' he chuckled. 'I came across your errant brother in the restaurant and dragged him home with me!'

'Perhaps it's best if I call back tomorrow,' said Max from behind them, while Abby sat frozen with shock.

'Don't be so ridiculous, Max,' exclaimed Jennifer sharply. 'It's hardly as though you don't know Abby.'

Even had she wanted to, Abby realised she couldn't have turned her head to see him—her every muscle had fused to solidity.

'Yes—and since you haven't graced us with your presence for long enough for us to get out our holiday snaps——' Paul grinned '—you can come and look at Abby's instead.'

'I'm amazed by your interest in them, Paul,' drawled Max. 'I wasn't aware you knew Abby.'

'I can't think why,' replied Paul, his puzzlement at his brother-in-law's tone creeping into his words. 'I've known Abby almost since she was a sprat. I just assumed you knew I was once engaged to her sister.'

'I didn't,' replied Max, his appearance round the side of the sofa visible even from Abby's rigidly fixed position. 'What a small world it is,' he added, stooping to kiss his sister.

'Max, you need a shave,' complained Jennifer affectionately. 'And you look dreadful,' she added with a note of concern, placing both her arms around his neck and giving him a sudden hug.

'Well, are we going to discuss my disgusting appearance or look at these photographs?' he demanded, lowering himself to a sitting position on the floor by his sister's feet. 'Hi, there, Abby,' he muttered, waving a languid hand in her direction.

'Hello,' managed Abby, though she would never know how.

He was dressed in dark trousers and loafers, and a bulky sweater he was in the process of removing as her eyes took their fill of him.

'It's like a furnace in here,' he complained, leaning his tousled head back against his sister's knee and proceeding to roll up the sleeves of his shirt.

'Stop whingeing,' ordered Jennifer, ruffling his hair, then passing the photographs over to Abby. 'Do your stuff, Abby.'

Attempting to talk her way through that handful of photographs proved to be one of the most daunting tasks ever asked of her. There wasn't just Paul's understandable puzzlement over her stammering lack of coherency, there was also the distracting matter of Jennifer's frequently barbed digs at her brother for her to contend with.

'It's about time you got married—thirty-one's getting on a bit, lover-boy,' needled Jennifer, while Abby busied herself putting the photographs in her bag and praying the ground would open up and swallow her.

'Who says I want to get married?' enquired Max, his head still comfortably nestled against his sister's legs and his eyes closed.

'I do,' retorted Jennifer. 'The only reason you sample so many women is because you're searching for a particular one... though I must say you seem to be having more trouble than most finding her,' she added waspishly.

'And I love you too, darling,' murmured Max, his tone almost drowsy. 'Jen, before I nod off and give you even more grounds for reminding me how uncouth I am, do you think you could rustle up some coffee?'

'Good idea,' said Paul, rising. 'I'll make it. Perhaps Abby would like to give me a hand?'

Abby glanced up at him in complete surprise. There was an unfamiliar grimness to his jaw that seemed to suggest suppressed anger.

'I don't mind giving you a hand in the least,' she said, her spirits at rock-bottom as she struggled to her feet. The atmosphere in the room was tense and loaded and she alone was responsible for it. Paul Lawson was perfectly capable of preparing a pot of coffee unassisted, but he obviously felt obliged to offer her an opportunity of a break in which to get a grip on herself. 'But I'll not stay for any—I really should be getting home.'

An almost light-headed sense of relief lurching through her, she made her way round the back of the sofa to where Jennifer was attempting to extricate herself from her brother's resting body.

'No—don't you get up, Jennifer,' she pleaded, forcing a smile to her lips.

'OK, I'll leave Paul to see you off,' murmured Jennifer, reaching back awkwardly to give Abby's arm a reassuring squeeze. 'But you be sure and give me a ring.'

'Of course I shall,' promised Abby. 'You and Paul must come to Kingston,' she added stiltedly.

'We'd love that. Drive carefully, Abby,' she warned. 'And I'm sure Max would wish you goodnight if he weren't asleep—or just plain ill-mannered.'

''Night, Abby,' was Max's lazy response to his sister's barbed prompt.

It was only when the door closed behind them that Abby realised Paul had taken her by the arm and led her from the room.

'It seems that old habits die hard,' he said quietly, 'and that I'm always going to regard you as a sort of kid sister who needs watching over.'

'That's very sweet of you, Paul,' muttered Abby, steeling herself for what was likely to come...though despairing of having the mental resources left to cope with his lecturing her on the obvious folly of getting involved with his brother-in-law. 'But I'm not in need of any watching over.'

'Oh, yes, you are,' he contradicted grimly. 'And if Jennifer doesn't succeed in extracting the reason why from Max, I most certainly intend to.'

'Max?' she exclaimed, forcing a puzzled frown to her face. 'What on earth has he to do with anything?' Her heart thudding as though it would burst, she glanced down at her watch, convinced that if she didn't get away now she would crack irreparably. 'I really must go—I have to be up rather early in the morning.'

She drove home with extreme care, acutely conscious of the potential danger of the state she was in, and it wasn't until she closed her own front door behind her that she let go, collapsing in an orgy of weeping despair.

Not that long ago she had been congratulating herself on being on the road to recovery, she remembered with bitterness, and now she had made a complete spectacle of herself. She had said nothing, admitted nothing...yet she might just as well have shouted her feelings from the rooftops for all the difference it would have made.

She stumbled up the stairs to her bedroom, her head filling with every nuance of expression that had flitted across those shadowed, handsome features, destroying her hope that her eyes hadn't betrayed her too often with the realisation they had more likely devoured him.

She stripped and stepped into the shower, the water cascading over her slim body doing nothing to cleanse her mind of the torment of its thoughts. Tonight's hostile stranger was the same man in whose arms she had once lain and whose fevered, ardent cries had filled her ears while his passion had filled her body, she reminded herself with the frantic intensity of one already beginning to question the trustworthiness of such memories.

It was no wonder she was reduced to such doubts, she told herself angrily, stepping from the shower and towelling herself dry with painful ferocity; she wasn't dealing with a normal man, but one callous to the point of depravity, and one who, despite everything they had once shared, now needed prompting from his sister even to show commonplace civility towards her!

But what of a woman who would squander love on such a creature? she demanded harshly of herself. Couldn't she also be accused of something bordering on depravity?

She flung on a nightdress, wrapped a towel round her still dripping hair and flounced down the stairs, her mind awash with self-recrimination.

Instead of calling him every low-down name he deserved, she had shrivelled and cowered like a pathetic creature unable to stand up for herself. But never again, she vowed, rubbing viciously against her wet hair with the towel. The next time he wouldn't know what had hit him as she verbally shredded him with her appraisal of his despicable nature. The next time... She froze mid-thought, dragging the towel from her head and telling herself it couldn't have been the doorbell she had heard. She glanced down at her wrist where her watch should have been and was trying to work how far past midnight it was when the doorbell rang again—this time a shrill, prolonged blast that indicated an impatient finger placed and left on the buzzer.

'Who is it?' she called out as she sped to the door.

'Max.'

'Go to hell!'

He replaced his finger on the buzzer.

'I'll call the police!'

'You can call whoever you like, Abby, but I'll have this bloody door kicked in long before anyone gets here!'

Her fury exacerbated by the knowledge that he wouldn't think twice before carrying out such a threat, she opened the door the merest of fractions.

'If you...' Her words deteriorated into a shriek of outrage as the door flew from her grasp and Max strode past her and off down the hallway.

'How dare you barge in here like this?' she yelled, letting the door swing closed then racing down the hallway and into the living-room after him. 'Get out of here!'

He swung round to face her, his eyes blazing.

'You left early and missed all the fun,' he snarled, 'so I've come to fill you in on all the gory details.'

'The last thing I wanted was for Jennifer and Paul to be dragged in to this...this sordid little saga!' she hurled at him, deciding that if he insisted on staying he would be the one on the receiving end of any gory details.

'And whose fault is it that it was so sordid?' he roared. 'You're the one who gloated over playing me at my own game!'

'Whose fault was it?' she exploded, ruthlessly ignoring the small stab of discomfort brought about by that unwelcome reminder as fury consumed her. 'You're the one who called all the shots, Max! You're the one who cold-bloodedly set out to get what you wanted from me and succeeded—and now you seem to want jam on it by implying it was all my fault anyway!'

'What did I do, Abby?' he demanded harshly. 'Tie you up and take you by force?'

'You tied me up, all right! You tied me up in such mental knots that in the end all you had to do was snap your fingers—— '

'In the end?' he queried coldly. 'It was right at the beginning that I seem to remember pointing out that either of us could have had the other on a plate if we so chose.'

'I don't care who said what when!' she almost screamed at him. 'You won! Your tactics were brilliant! But don't you ever dare to try loading off on me any blame for the outcome of your tacky philandering—not ever!'

For an instant he looked as though he was about to hurl a barrage of abuse at her, then his expression faltered as he dragged his fingers through his hair in a gesture of helpless bemusement.

'One of us has to belong on another planet,' he groaned, walking over to an armchair and flinging himself down on it in sprawling weariness. 'Just what the hell did you think was going on in my mind?' he demanded, scowling up at her.

'I don't know. I've never had any idea what's gone on in your mind and, what's more, I no longer have the slightest wish to do so.'

'Yet you obviously haven't let that minor consideration deter you from judging me.'

'Once you could have tied me up in knots with that sort of word play,' she accused, edging towards the sofa on legs threatening to buckle under her, yet loath to sit down for fear of creating an impression of encouraging his presence by so doing, 'but not any more.'

'While we're on this subject of knots that so preoccupies you,' he muttered, ramming his hands in his pockets and sliding further down into the chair as he stretched his legs out before him, 'there are a few I'd like unravelled.' He glanced up, his only apparent reaction, as she finally sat down, one of mild irritation at having been momentarily distracted. 'Such as why you denied all knowledge of Paul when I asked if you knew him.'

She gazed across at his scowling face and felt a rush of relief that she actually had given in and sat down.

'I suppose this is another of your convoluted jokes,' she accused, feeling suddenly drained as her mind refused even to attempt puzzling out what he could be up to.

He gave her a look she found so impossible to interpret that she was left wondering if her mind hadn't stopped functioning altogether—or, perhaps, his.

'No—but I'm beginning to wonder if it isn't one of yours,' he muttered. 'And you still haven't told me why you denied knowing Paul.'

'I wasn't aware that I had.'

'You did.'

Still completely at a loss as to what his intentions could be, she nevertheless began casting her mind back over the weeks in search of an answer, prompted by the unnatural stillness in his body as he sat there watching and waiting, as though coiled to spring should she fail to supply one.

'You're right—I did,' she muttered, her memory at last responding. 'It was just easier than explaining—I was a bit confused over things at the time.'

'Confused over what things?'

She hesitated, tempted to tell him to mind his own business and order him out, but then leaned further back against the sofa, accepting it would be a waste of breath.

'When Paul said he was once engaged to my sister, he was leaving out a lot—it wasn't nearly as straightforward as that,' she began. 'Our parents had been killed in a road accident less than a year before Elaine and Paul met and, though I was far too young to realise it, she was in no mental state to embark on any romantic relationship. Without any awareness on her part, or his, for a long time, she used him as an emotional crutch.'

'Obviously he let her.'

'It wasn't a question of his *letting* her,' she protested. 'Paul is a deeply caring man and he was very fond of Elaine, but I don't think he had the slightest idea what love really was until he met Jennifer. By the time he and Elaine had slipped into being engaged—without, I should point out, his actually ever having proposed to her—he was desperately worried about her and had realised that, despite the years that had by then passed since our parents' death, she needed professional counselling.'

'And did he arrange for her to get it?'

Abby shook her head. 'I know he tried... but by then he had met and fallen in love with Jennifer and Elaine refused even to speak to him once he had told her... Eventually she moved to Canada and gradually recovered.'

'None of this explains why you should deny knowing him several years later,' he observed coolly.

'Doesn't it?' she snapped, rattled by his coolness. He was the one who had demanded to hear all this and she the one obliging, despite not having the slightest idea why. 'I hated Paul. I blamed him for the heartache Elaine had suffered and which had driven her to Canada. I'd no idea who Jennifer was when I got my job with Bradley Designs, but I felt my whole world was disintegrating around me when I first saw Paul at the offices and learned the truth.'

'I'm afraid you've lost me completely,' he said in cold, almost clinically detached tones.

'I felt I was betraying my sister by working where I was... I couldn't even bring myself to write to her and tell her the truth, though it later turned out she already knew. And when Paul tried to speak to me, I refused—I wanted nothing to do with him.'

'If that's the case, how was it I once opened the door to your office and found you in his arms?'

Abby froze; there was no mistaking the implication in his words.

'You...I don't believe this,' she floundered. 'You thought I was...what...? Having an affair with Paul?'

'I soon found out that, whatever it was, it wasn't an affair.'

She tried in vain to close her mind to the welter of images bombarding it, a debilitating lethargy trembling through her as a pattern slowly formed from the confusions that had so long engulfed her.

'Oh, you found out all right,' she whispered raggedly. 'All those times I actually tried kidding myself it wasn't dislike I kept seeing in your eyes...but that's far too mild a word for what you must have been feeling towards the woman you'd judged to be harming your sister...the woman you'd decided to teach a lesson she would never forget!'

'Abby, perhaps there was a time when I wanted to punish you,' he groaned, rubbing his hands wearily across his stubbled chin. 'But it wasn't as simple as that.'

'How much more simple do you need it?' she croaked, her voice breaking.

'For God's sake, Abby, I'm trying to be honest with you, which is something I've never felt you've been with me! I admit I got it all wrong about you and Paul... but you *were* hiding something from me... Damn it, Abby, I *know* you were!'

'Of course I was hiding something from you,' she conceded defeatedly, turning and burying her face against the wing of the sofa as she tried desperately to cling on to what was left of her rapidly dwindling control.

'Something so terrible that you couldn't even share it with the only man with whom you have ever made love?' he asked sadly, rising.

'I tried to explain once,' she choked. 'I told you I was afraid of falling in love with you and all you did was sneer!'

'I expressed an identical fear that night we went out with the Morrisons,' he retorted angrily. 'And I don't remember crowing about what a ludicrous idea it was, the way you did, nor claiming it was a fear mercifully behind me!'

Cowed by the almost palpable anger emanating from him, she buried her face deeper against the cushioned surface as the last of her defences crumbled. What was she supposed to do—admit that it was her love she had been hiding from him?

'Abby, please... don't,' he whispered, his hand tentatively patting against her leg as he strode over and crouched before her. 'Forgive me... I had no right to come here and behave like this after all I've put you through.'

'Why did you, then?' she choked brokenly, no longer caring what she did or said.

'Because I was desperate to try to unravel this hideous mess that's been in my head for so long now that I can scarcely remember what sanity is.'

She straightened slightly, her tear-washed eyes at first accusing as they gazed down into his darkly drawn face, then haunted as love rekindled within her, blazing with an intensity that threatened to suffocate her.

'Abby, if you saw dislike in my eyes...there must have been other things you saw,' he pleaded.

'Stop it,' she begged, ruthlessly stifling the memory of the hope that had once surged in her. 'I could never understand the way you were...but I can now!'

'Can you?' he demanded, changing his crouched position at her feet to a sitting one. 'How can you know of the conversation that took place between my sister and me even before I started using her office?'

'Max, what's the point of any of this?' she pleaded wearily, the effort of fighting the need to reach out and hold him draining her.

'Let me have my say and then ask me that,' he pleaded softly.

She closed her eyes in silent acquiescence, her body tense and rigid as it huddled into the corner of the sofa.

'Jennifer was livid with me tonight. She told me I was a crazy, muddle-headed lunatic and that she would never forgive me unless I got myself sorted out.'

So that was what all this was about, thought Abby with a stomach-churning bitterness; she was being subjected to this excruciating torture simply so that he could get back into his sister's good books.

'And that if I didn't,' he continued, 'she would probably spend the rest of her life riddled with guilt.'

'Why on earth should she feel any guilt?' demanded Abby. 'She's not responsible for the way you behave.'

'Of course she's not,' he retorted impatiently. 'It's just that... hell, Abby, I'd no idea that some women can get a bit emotionally disorientated during the early stages of pregnancy,' he exclaimed wearily. 'All I do know is that one day I went round to see Jennifer and found her in the most alarming state. She started rambling on about her marriage standing no chance and then seemed to link it up with Paul having been engaged when they met. She then switched her ramblings to you—saying that nothing could ever be the same between herself and Paul now that you'd turned up again.'

'I don't... I mean... this is crazy!' protested Abby distractedly. 'Jennifer did tell me tonight that she'd had this crazy fixation that... Why didn't you ask me about any of this?' she cried out in a howl of bemused outrage. 'How could you have believed... what exactly *did* you believe, for heaven's sake?'

'I honestly don't know,' he admitted defeatedly. 'I got it into my head that you'd been engaged to him... but that didn't really fit as you'd have been extremely young.'

'So why didn't you ask Jennifer?'

'In any other circumstances I would have—even though she'd made it plain soon after her outburst that she was embarrassed by it and wanted us both to forget it—but as things were, I decided to leave well alone.'

'You could have asked Paul,' she plugged on, defying the voice crying out in her that enough was enough.

'Apart from the fact that I've never had any doubts about his feelings for Jennifer, I knew that she would consider it an unforgivable breach of confidence if I were to say anything to him.'

'My God, I don't believe this!' she croaked weakly. 'You had no doubts about his feelings for your sister at the same time as believing he and I were having an affair!'

'Yes...no! Hell, Abby, don't ask me to explain something I'm unable to understand myself!'

'Yet you understood exactly what you were doing when you set out to punish me,' she accused, the harshness of a mortal hurt in her words.

'For an intelligent woman you can be incredibly stupid at times! I was punishing myself every bit as much as I was you!' he rounded on her furiously. 'You...' He broke off, shaking his head dejectedly. 'Abby, darling, I'm sorry,' he whispered hoarsely. 'I'm trying not to lose my temper...but I just can't seem to make you understand.'

His apology, the spontaneous way he had called her 'darling', and most of all the terrible desperation in his tone were all ganging up on her, reawakening memories of all those sweet, incomprehensible moments that had torn aside her defences and led to her loving him and which now threatened to rip her apart.

'Abby, having been wrong about Paul for all those years, how did it feel suddenly learning the truth?'

'It's not the same,' she protested; then, hearing the terrible uncertainty in her tone, added bitterly, 'I hadn't set out to destroy Paul for what I felt he'd done to Elaine.'

'Abby, you've got to believe me!' he pleaded hoarsely, then exploded in exasperation. 'How can I get through to you? All right—just tell me how you would have felt if Paul had had a brother you were in danger of falling in love with...who, despite everything you tried, you did fall in love with.'

With no consciousness of what she was doing, she leaned forward, her eyes instinctively searching out the truth they would find in his.

'Oh, yes,' he whispered softly, his eyes telling her things her reason ordered her to reject, 'at last I'm beginning to get through.' He reached over and took her clenched hands in his, his fingers gently prising hers open and interlacing themselves among them. 'Abby, the first time I looked into those unforgettable green eyes of yours I had a premonition of what was about to happen to me and I fought it with everything I had. But when my need for just one word of explanation from you became an obsession that overrode my feelings of betrayal towards Jennifer, I was scared out of my wits. Now tonight I've learned that I'd wasted all that time begging for an explanation to something that had simply never existed.' He sighed, the stubble of his chin sharp against her fingers as he pressed their entwined hands to his face. 'Is it any wonder that I'm still in the throes of a complete brainstorm?'

'Max,' she whispered softly, the love within her hurling aside a multitude of doubts as it soared to freedom.

'No!' he protested, shaking his head fiercely. 'Whatever you think, you've got to believe that I love you... that I've been fighting it one moment, desperately trying to give it a chance the next, and so eaten up by it for so long now that I can't remember a time when I was free of it.'

For an instant she felt her heart stop, then it began pounding as though it would burst.

'How can I be expected to believe that from a man in the throes of a brainstorm?' she asked in a peculiarly strained voice, while the cobwebs of confusion began drifting from her mind.

The indignation burning in his eyes, as they rose to hers, faltered before blazing into incredulous delight. He tore his hands free of hers, then dragged her down into his arms, their tumbling bodies clinging instantly.

'There's a simple cure for this brainstorm of mine,' he groaned, his lips showering her face with frantic, insatiable kisses. 'Just tell me you love me.'

'You know I love you,' she gasped, unable to tell whether it was his arms or simply her own mind-blowing happiness that was making breathing so difficult.

'Tell me!'

'I love you. I *was* afraid of loving you, for a short while... but what I spent so long trying to hide from you was that I did love you—that I do love you,' she choked, her lips pressing their own fevered kisses of welcome wherever they could. 'Max, if only you knew how much I love you.'

'The rest of our lives should be just about long enough for me to start getting the idea,' he whispered passionately. 'That is if you can ever forgive me enough to consider putting up with me for that long after what I've put you through with my pig-headed blindness... Abby, my darling, can you ever forgive me?'

'I might just manage to... at some point in the rest of our lives,' she teased, only to find the breath jarring in her lungs as her body responded with uninhibited delight to the hands now committedly exploring it.

'At some time in the rest of our lives *together*,' he corrected huskily. 'Will you marry me?' he whispered, his hands now trespassing unrestrainedly.

'Yes,' she choked, and it was all the speech she was capable of as the combination of a surfeit of happiness and the sensuous effect of his hands took its ecstatic toll on her.

'I hope you're not going to insist on champagne at our wedding,' he murmured distractedly as her hands enthusiastically began following the example of his. 'I've never been able to face the stuff since that terrible day in Cornwall...' His words deteriorated to a stifled chuckle of contentment as her mouth silenced his with its impassioned suggestion that his recent aversion to champagne was a matter they could afford to leave on ice for the time being.

Next Month's Romances

Each month you can choose from a wide variety of romance with Mills & Boon. Below are the new titles to look out for next month, why not ask either Mills & Boon Reader Service or your Newsagent to reserve you a copy of the titles you want to buy – just tick the titles you would like and either post to Reader Service or take it to any Newsagent and ask them to order your books.

Please save me the following titles:		Please tick ✓
THE WEDDING	Emma Darcy	
LOVE WITHOUT REASON	Alison Fraser	
FIRE IN THE BLOOD	Charlotte Lamb	
GIVE A MAN A BAD NAME	Roberta Leigh	
TRAVELLING LIGHT	Sandra Field	
A HEALING FIRE	Patricia Wilson	
AN OLD ENCHANTMENT	Amanda Browning	
STRANGERS BY DAY	Vanessa Grant	
CONSPIRACY OF LOVE	Stephanie Howard	
FIERY ATTRACTION	Emma Richmond	
RESCUED	Rachel Elliot	
DEFIANT LOVE	Jessica Hart	
BOGUS BRIDE	Elizabeth Duke	
ONE SHINING SUMMER	Quinn Wilder	
TRUST TOO MUCH	Jayne Bauling	
A TRUE MARRIAGE	Lucy Gordon	

If you would like to order these books in addition to your regular subscription from Mills & Boon Reader Service please send £1.80 per title to: Mills & Boon Reader Service, Freepost, P.O. Box 236, Croydon, Surrey, CR9 9EL, quote your Subscriber No:.............................. (If applicable) and complete the name and address details below. Alternatively, these books are available from many local Newsagents including W.H.Smith, J.Menzies, Martins and other paperback stockists from 10 September 1993.

Name:..

Address:..

....Post Code:.......................

To Retailer: If you would like to stock M&B books please contact your regular book/magazine wholesaler for details.

You may be mailed with offers from other reputable companies as a result of this application. If you would rather not take advantage of these opportunities please tick box ☐